I0451511

The Corner Saloon

By Arline Fisher

PROLOGUE

Philip ran the keyboard, not hearing anything too much out of tune. The dust, the altitude and the total lack of humidity took its toll on even the finest instrument. Oh, how he had cursed his mother for the hours spent practicing at the old upright piano in their parlor, but it only took a few days operating a sluice box to make him appreciate the talent in his hands. He shot his cuffs, checked his cufflinks and made sure his nails were clean. His clientele appreciated such things. There were times he wished one of the performers at the opera house would notice him and invite him on tour; he longed to see the fabled San Francisco. For now, however, he would have to content himself with the vantage point he enjoyed looking over Virginia City in its heyday. There were worse jobs, he knew from experience.

……..

Juliette buffed her nails to a shine, each one a perfect crescent moon shape. She found that her customers appreciated this little dignity as much as they liked her perfume and her long curls. She thought back to the days of working "the line" in the tent shacks at the bottom of the C Street hill. Then it was a struggle even to keep her hair clean; fingernails were a luxury worn away by dragging endless stained sheets across the laundry washboards. As a house girl her life had improved so much, and anything she could do to maintain her status was well worth it. In such a rough crowd it might have been surprising, but she had become an expert at reading men and knew they liked to escape the dirt and find some comfort with a clean, perfumed, extravagantly coiffed woman, even if she was just a whore.

……..

Jack dragged the pristine white towel across the bar, thinking that by night's end there would probably be two-bits worth of whiskey in it, but it could be worse. He could be down the street at the Bucket of Blood where the bar towel — if they had one — would have sopped up more whiskey, more beer, and likely some blood as well. Every knuckle on his hands was broken from the years he worked down there, breaking up fights as often as pouring drinks. The two blocks distance between the Bucket and The Corner Saloon represented a world of difference. The Corner Saloon had a hat-check girl and a shoeshine stand, and before dawn every day a crew of Chinese would come in to scrub and polish the oak floors by hand. Although there weren't blood stains and spit to contend with, the dirt streets made it a constant challenge to keep anything clean.

……..

Padraig wrapped a bit of rag around his right hand and switched the pick to his left. Eight hours a day, six days a week in the tunnels had turned his hands to cracked leather, but even after nearly a year of the backbreaking labor, they still bled. This work made digging for potatoes in Ireland look like child's play, he thought, but still he was so much better off. At least he and his family had food. If his wife shrunk from his touch at night because of his rough hands, he knew she was grateful for the steady work, even if she worried about his safety in the mines; tunnels did collapse and kill the miners inside on a regular basis. Recently an organization had formed to provide something for the widows of miners. E. Clampus Vitus, they were named, or simply "The Clampers." Their red shirts and raucous initiation ceremonies were fast becoming the stuff of legends. Padraig laughed at the stories but put a few bits in their collection box whenever he could.

……..

From the comfort of The Corner Saloon next to the famed Piper's Opera House, gentlemen could just as easily watch the pomp and glamour associated with the arrival of the latest Shakespearean troupe as oversee the shuffling march of a new gang of Chinese "coolies" destined for the mines. Men with names like Stanford, Huntington and Mackay watched as Virginia City made them rich beyond even their East Coast counterparts. While much of their wealth was put back into the mines and railroads serving the Comstock Lode, they also created the more genteel and sophisticated San Francisco some 200 miles to the west. But their real excitement came from Virginia City, a ramshackle collection of homes, thousands of tents, businesses fronting planked boardwalks, a hundred or so saloons, a few schools, and even a dozen churches—all atop a silver vein larger than any could have imagined.

Book One

Drawn West

Philip

1.

Farming would never be in Philip's blood, he was certain. His father had been overjoyed to learn of the government's Homestead Act offering 160 acres free of charge to those who would agree to farm the Great Plains and was quick to bundle the family into a wagon heading west. The grinding sameness of it all, the flat unremarkable land, the ceaseless wind and the backbreaking chores, the same every day, weighed on Philip, a young man of 18. His father urged him to apply for his own plat of land, but Philip would not. He missed their home in Boston. He missed his friends and had no real opportunity to make any new ones isolated as they were on their farm. The highlight of the week, if he could call it that, was the family outing to church on Sundays where Philip played the piano for the faltering choir.

Philip had unenthusiastically attended school in Boston as far as the tenth grade, but his father's rash decision to transport them west had been the end of that. At first Philip was relieved but gradually came to resent having his education cut short, reducing his prospects in life to manual labor, in this case, farming. His father relished hooking up their horse to a plow and spending all day walking behind it, instructing Philip to break up the larger clods with a shovel. He trod along behind his father and the plow wishing he was strolling on the Boston waterfront with his friends, stealing an occasional piece of fruit from the stands run by the Italians. How they laughed to see the Italian grocer trying to chase them, waving his fist and shouting until he was red in the face! There was very little laughter on the farm. Even his younger brothers and sisters worked all day, clearing rocks, tending to the chickens, milking the cows, trying to start a small garden. When they invented little games, they were short-lived before they got a stern warning from father or mother to return to their chores. There was a special kind of meanness out here, Philip thought, noting that even the sun seemed dragged down, obscured as it was by a layer of swirling dust almost all the time.

For the first two years they lived in little more than a dug-out in the side of a hill, the front wall made of stacked sod. Ma cried all the time, it seemed, overwhelmed by the unrelenting dirt and dust. She, too, was remembering their small home in Boston with its brick walls and wood floors. They even had a parlor with an upright piano. She taught piano lessons and insisted that Philip learn as well. When father announced that the family was to go west, every pretty, delicate thing she owned was left behind. Her mother's china set was sold to a neighbor for just a few dollars. The local seamstress bought her fancy dresses, saying she intended to tear them apart to use the fabric on new frocks for her clients. She had no jewelry to speak of but at least kept her small gold wedding band. What they couldn't sell before they left was simply stacked in front of the house to be rifled through by the neighbors.

Ma's mother disapproved of the move but reminded Ma of her wedding vows, so at first she tried to put a brave face on the adventure, as she called it, engaging Philip and his siblings in studying the passing countryside. But, when they arrived on the Plains and his father staked out their new holdings, the yawning emptiness settled in; Ma thought she would lose her mind. Father would become frustrated with her constant crying or her silent reproach. Sometimes it would come to a violent end with father beating her, then being contrite and ashamed. "But damn woman! Can't you see how hard I'm working for all of us?" he would cry out in frustration.

After two years of unimaginable hard work and frustration, Philip's father announced that it was time to start work on a small house for the family and that Philip should prepare the wagon to go into town for lumber and other sundry supplies necessary for the building. The two of them set off for town one spring morning, leaving Ma and the other children to tend the farm. Philip noted each homestead they passed was as poor as their own, some even worse with no crops to speak of and perhaps only one cow. Their fellow farmers waved dispiritedly then bent back to their chores. A two-hour wagon ride brought them to the small town sprung up by the railroad tracks and they went immediately to the lumber yard where father haggled over every board, it seemed. When the wagon was loaded and the building supplies secured, Philip's father surprised him by saying that perhaps they could stop off at the saloon and have a beer to "wet their whistles" before they headed back to the farm. Philip had never been in a saloon and had never drank a beer, so this was quite a thrilling turn of events.

The saloon was little more than a ramshackle wood building with a tin roof and a makeshift bar along one side. A dozen or so tables filled the interior, about half of them occupied with farmers and travelers waiting for the train's imminent departure. Philip's father chose a table nearer to the farmers but Philip himself strained to hear what the train passengers had to say about where they were going. Almost to a man the answer was Virginia City in the Nevada Territory. "I've heard every little hill is just a mound of silver," one said, and another agreed, "It's bigger than the Gold Rush, I'll tell you." Philip was enthralled but too afraid of his father's reaction to ask more about this Virginia City. He vowed to come back to the saloon the first chance he got.

2.

Little by little Philip and his father made progress on the house while Philip's younger brother, William, took on more responsibility for the farm work. Ma watched hopefully and cried less often, although she was still overcome at times thinking of everything she had left behind. The 160-acre parcels made it virtually impossible to visit with neighbors, and she and the children remained quite isolated; at least Philip and father made occasional trips to town. The weekly family trip to the little church built at the edge of town was over way too quickly for Ma. Sometimes they would stay on and have a little Sunday potluck meal with the other farmers, but often as not father would insist that they return home and get in a few more hours' work on the house before dark.

When it came time to harvest their first successful wheat crop, father deemed it necessary to work side-by-side with William, so the work on the house fell increasingly to Philip. He was secretly pleased to be let out of the boring, back-breaking farm labor and began to take pride in building the house. He hoped to please Ma by suggesting little improvements to make the house more than just a 3-room box. The addition of a porch along the entire front of the house was one such improvement that Philip engineered as well as the digging out of a root cellar off the back of the house. At first Ma protested, thinking the cellar would become infested with the ever present mice and gophers, but Philip convinced her the convenience of being able to store food — well-sealed, of course — would overcome her concerns, and — maybe they could get a cat or a dog to run off the varmints. The littler children would love that!

Of course, Philip had an ulterior motive for these improvements. Each change or addition gave him the opportunity to go to the hardware store in town where he became quite well-known. "So, you're still working on the palace, are you?" the proprietor would tease him. "Got those towers and that solid copper roof on yet?" Philip laughed easily and assured the older man that there might be even more grandiose plans in the works. They soon developed such a rapport that he could leave the wagon and his list of supplies for the man to fill, then head straight to the saloon by the railroad tracks.

The bartender came to know Philip as well. By cutting a few corners here and there on the house supplies, Philip usually had enough money for a beer or two, allowing him to sit for a few hours and listen to the railroad passengers talk about their travels. More than a few were gold miners returning from California with little more than dust in their pockets, and there were farmers who fought against the plains but failed to produce a crop and now had to return to where they'd come from, in poverty and shame. But it was the men heading west who captured Philip's attention. He'd look for any excuse to approach them with a query. "Do you expect you'll be opening your own mine?" he'd ask, "Or are there jobs in the mines for someone not quite so well-set as yourself?" They were happy to share their opinions about what awaited them in Virginia City, and of course, when one started talking about the silver there, others joined in.

On one such afternoon Philip noticed an addition to the saloon, an old upright piano similar to what his family had owned in Boston. He ran his hand over the keys and heard it was terribly out of tune. The bartender told him someone had found it out on the plains and had traded it to him for four beers. Philip opened the top and borrowed a bar rag to clean the inside as much as possible, tightening and adjusting the piano wires until it was at least playable. Without any sheet music, he sat down and had to play from memory, but after a few songs the customers clapped and a couple dropped a few bits down next to him on the piano bench. It became a pattern. Every week or two Philip needed more supplies for the house and escaped to play piano in the saloon.

The bartender took him aside one day. "Say, what if you was to play the piano here Friday and Saturday nights, sort of liven things up a bit? I could probably give you a couple dollars every night and whatever the customers give you would be yours to keep."

Philip was flattered but his shoulders sunk when he replied. "Well, sir, thank you, but I live so far out of town and all…"

"Oh, I know you do, boy. You'd wear out those old horses coming in here that often." He took a sip of his own beer, "I could arrange it so you hitched a ride on the mail coach coming into town, same way going back." He hesitated a bit before adding, "What if I give you a room upstairs for those nights and you could take your meals out back with the whores?"

Philip didn't know which was more exciting—playing the piano for money or the fact that there were whores he could take his meals with. "I'd have to ask my father," he stammered, "but yes, sir, I'd surely enjoy that!" He could have run all the way home without the wagon as excited as he was to share the news about this opportunity. He used the two-hour ride to frame his argument, thinking the best course might be to emphasize the extra money it would bring to the family. And William was doing the farming anyhow. One thing he wouldn't mention was that he would secretly begin saving for a train ticket to Virginia City. And, he wouldn't mention the whores.

3.

It was a helluva fight but in the end Philip's mother settled it. "The boy needs to get off this miserable lonely farm now and then!" She glared at his father. "Bad enough the rest of us are stuck out here with no one but ourselves to talk to." And even though she knew she'd won, she couldn't help adding, "I wish they'd asked *me*!" Philip's father looked ready to explode and his mother knew it. With a flick of her skirts and a toss of her curly red hair, she laughed and announced, "Why I might even have danced on the tables for them." The youngest children laughed and begged her to do just that and eventually father took her in his arms for a little turn around the floor. Soon everyone was dancing and laughing, a rare moment indeed.

Philip was never so grateful for his mother's love. He took after her emotionally, he knew, being moved by a beautiful sunset or the call of geese flying overhead, and it was she, of course, who had instilled his love of music. His hair was a lighter shade of red than hers, with blonde-gold streaks, but he had the same long tapering fingers and slight build, although he was tall at nearly six feet. In contrast, William was an exact duplicate of father—a solid build, thick black hair and a perpetually brooding expression, nearly a scowl. His thick hands and broad back were adaptable to the farm work for certain. He was happy to hear that Philip would be gone for at least part of the week.

In the days leading up to the next Friday Philip worked like a dervish around the house, finishing the railing on the porch and attending to a hundred small details. Friday morning found him standing at the side of the road awaiting the mail coach. His mother had fretted that he did not have a decent white shirt for his "debut," as she called it, but she had made him clean his nails and trimmed his hair for him. "Now, be sure to sit up straight when you're playing," she admonished him, "and smile! You have such a beautiful smile." Father simply told him to watch out for his money and be sure the bartender paid him every night, no credit.

When the coach pulled up, Philip clambered up next to the driver, who offered his hand and introduced himself as Riley. "So, you're the new pie-anna player," he drawled. "Bout time we got some class in that place, I guess." Riley was a natural-born gossip and had a story about each farmstead they passed—which farmer was a drunk, which farm wife might be too free with her affections, and which farm might be only a season away from failure, and there were several of those. Philip enjoyed the ride and the colorful conversation and made plans to meet up with Riley for the return trip on Sunday, although he supposed he could just have easily gone to church and ridden home with his family.

What he had done for free on many an afternoon now seemed like a daunting task to Philip, approaching the piano with some trepidation. Jake the bartender plunked a beer down in front of him and told him to just relax; he didn't really have to play until the train came in anyway. Philip sipped his beer and nodded to some of the regulars, and he wondered, just where were the whores? Finally, the train whistle could be heard in the distance, so Philip finished his beer and set to playing a snappy little waltz. He would have to ask around to see if anyone had any sheet music tucked away as his 10-song repertoire was bound to wear thin, especially as about half of those were hymns.

The train disgorged its usual assortment of grizzled miners, worn-out farmers with their families and a few traveling salesmen. The farmers lingered outside the saloon but the others made their way in directly. The train crew would rest up for two hours before setting off to the east. The next day, the same pattern would repeat in reverse but this time with fortune-seekers heading for the mines, farmers hoping to stake their claim, and another contingent of salesmen. Philip did notice that several of the crew members headed directly upstairs, probably to sleeping rooms, he thought, although from the sounds of laughter and other noises overhead, Philip finally deduced that was the location of the whores; he played the piano just a bit louder.

When the train pulled out, the local residents began to drift in, some standing at the bar to talk a bit with Jake, others heading for tables where some played cards but mostly just talked about the war, about farming, and about who was planning to head out west. Philip wished he could join in the conversations but he was able to hear enough bits and pieces to make out the general sadness and unease over the Civil

War balanced by the excitement of a new adventure and possible fortune to be found in the West.

Later that evening Philip volunteered to help Jake sweep up the bar and empty the spittoons, an offer Jake accepted gladly. He pulled two dollars out of the till and handed them to Philip, adding to the six bits in tips he had made that afternoon. The traveling salesmen were the most generous with their money, Philip saw.

"Let's get you bunked down," Jake said, gesturing for Philip to follow him upstairs. "And I imagine you're a mite hungry by now, too." Philip's stomach growled in response, making both men laugh. After being shown a small room with a single bed and a wash basin, Philip followed Jake down back staircase that opened into a dining room/lounge. And here were the whores! Philip blushed down to his toes at their catcalls, wondering who the new boy was and where did he get that beautiful red hair? One was so bold as to run her fingers through it, exclaiming, "Why it's like spun gold! Or red silk from China." The others laughed and continued to tease him until Jake told them to settle down and put a plate of stew in front of Philip. He ate like a starved man, which he almost was. Then, not knowing what else to do, he excused himself.

"Good night…ladies," he coughed. More taunts followed but he managed to get up and back to his room without embarrassing himself further. He thought he would be too excited to sleep, but he was wrong.

4.

Word spread that there was some fun to be had at Jake's saloon on Friday and Saturday nights with the addition of a new piano player. The whores were encouraged to come downstairs and mingle, sometimes even dance with the customers, so it was a lively place. Philip did get new sheet music from a widower when he cleaned out his wife's what-nots. Tips improved and Jake even agreed to pay Philip an extra dollar each weekend, money he dutifully took home to his parents, but keeping the tip money for himself.

Having his own spending money presented Philip with a dilemma. He certainly would have liked to have taken one of the whores upstairs but then he weighed those few minutes of pleasure against the weeks and weeks it took to earn the tips and the longer he would have to wait to head to Virginia City. Several of the girls had offered Philip a free taste, as it were, but Jake soon put an end to that. Still, seeing the girls flounce around the saloon with their hair done up and their colorful dresses somewhat made up for it. He couldn't imagine these girls out in the drab little house on the plains and sometimes he wondered if his little sisters would be stuck out there, too. Not that he wanted them to become whores, of course.

The extra money Philip earned did indeed make a difference in his family's life. He was able to take home some window shutters and a little can of green paint one week. His mother painted the shutters and Philip hung them. They did brighten the house up from the outside and provided some relief from the incessant wind. His father was able to buy extra seed and put more land in cultivation, and by expanding their garden they could make a little extra money by selling fresh produce to their neighbors. What they didn't sell, they canned, a chore the younger sisters delighted in. The colorful jars of beans and pickles, berries and even a few apples from two scrawny trees were carefully tucked into the root cellar like money in the bank. Philip's family would be one of the ones that would survive, even thrive, on the Great Plains. His father and brother were content and if the women were not, well, there was nothing to be done about it.

Over the last year Philip had been dropping what he hoped were subtle references into the dinner conversations about what he had heard about Virginia City and the riches to be made. His father always harrumphed and often as not told Philip those were just exaggerations designed to lure a bunch of fools to their end. But Philip's mother was listening more closely, so it came as no great surprise to her when Philip announced his plans to take the train west the following week. Again, there was a fierce argument about his need to stay and help the family, but again Philip's mother prevailed. "A longing for something exciting is just natural in a young man," she told his father. "Look how you longed to come out here and try your hand at a new life." He admitted as much and swelled with pride when she added, "And look how well you've done and how happy we are." After a bit, both parents agreed that it was time for Philip to strike out on his own and see once and for all if this Virginia City would be his dream. They didn't take the wagon to town the day he left, but they listened for the train whistle when he left.

5. Juliette

Juliette's father doted on her. How he loved to see her dark auburn curls stretching halfway down her back and her turquoise blue eyes. She was a delicate girl but a serious child, too. That part she got from her mother, no doubt, who was a strong believer in education and made certain Juliette attended the best girls' school. And books. He had never seen anyone who loved books as much as Juliette. She liked her pretty dolls and stylish dresses, but when he left for the bank every morning she had the same request, "Oh, papa, do see if there are any new books in the market, please." She'd flutter her eyelashes and throw herself around his neck. "I love you, papa. One new book, please, please, please." She was impossible to resist.

They lived in a stately brick home in a charming neighborhood in London just a few blocks from the bank where he had been president for nearly 20 years. The house was furnished comfortably but not ostentatiously. Silk lamp shades cast a pleasing pattern over velvet couches and a settee shipped all the way from India. She and her mother wore delicate hand-embroidered silk slippers when they were in the house. Juliette's room was half dollhouse, half library. She had her own little reading nook which she shared with an assortment of dolls. But all of that was gone in an afternoon when Juliette's father, accused of embezzlement, apparently rightfully so, shot and killed himself at his desk.

The very next day officers of the bank pounded on the front door. The grieving widow was shocked to hear they had only an hour to gather what they could carry and vacate the house. Juliette and her mother were sobbing as they each packed a bag. Juliette's mother put a dress, her best shoes, a sewing kit and the family Bible into her bag; Juliette packed her books, one small doll and her winter coat. Before leaving their home, however, she left the doll behind and took her Sunday shoes instead.

Juliette and her mother stood on the sidewalk at a complete loss. Where would they go now? No one in the neighborhood would help them, of course, after the scandal with the bank. Her mother held her head up high and admonished Juliette to do the same as they walked out of their neighborhood and down toward the wharves, the poor industrial part of town. Toward twilight they chanced upon a sign indicating rooms to let and that evening found them in two shabby rooms in the meatpacking district. Both of them felt they had given up everything pretty, although Juliette found comfort in her cherished books and her mother in the Bible.

Juliette could no longer attend school, of course, due to their "reduced circumstances," so she took to wandering the streets and nearby markets, book in hand, observing the commerce and the people who conducted it. She thought perhaps one day she would write about all the characters, a class of people who were entirely new and foreign to her. When the owner of one of the larger meat markets saw her one day with a book, he inquired of her, "Can you read, miss?"

"Well, of course, I can," she replied incredulously. "I was the top of my class at Miss Simmons' School," she boasted, but then dropped her head. "I can't go there any longer, sir." He asked where she lived and a few days later came to their door, asking if she could tutor his son in reading. It was a godsend for Juliette and her mother who had taken in sewing to make even a little bit of money. They agreed that he would send for her three afternoons a week in exchange for a shilling, each session.

The meatpacker's son was a spoiled, horrible little child, Juliette decided immediately upon meeting him. Charles refused to sit still and balked at reading even a line out of his primer. Flattery was of no use with him either, as he considered everything his due. "You must show me how well you read," Juliette coaxed.

"I musn't do anything I don't care to do," he defied her. It went on like that for two full sessions until Juliette entered the drawing room, made herself comfortable and opened a book of her own. Within minutes she was smiling and laughing to herself.

"Let me see. Let me read it," Charles clamored.

"Oh, you wouldn't care for this," Juliette said, then went back to reading and laughing to herself. "Oh, my!"

It was finally too much for the boy and he snatched the book out of her hands. He pretended to read it and then threw it down. "I don't see as there is anything funny in that."

"Well, perhaps if I read a bit to you…?" She patted the bench next to her and he grudgingly took a seat there. She began to read to him and pointed out words as she went, then asked him to do the same. He began haltingly but gradually became more confident. At the end of their session he was smiling and implored her to bring that same book with her the next time she came. His father had been watching the tableau and seemed pleased as well, offering her a ride home in his carriage. When they passed his market, he signaled the driver to stop, jumped out and disappeared into the market, returning with a small wrapped parcel which he gave to her along with the three shillings she had earned that week. The parcel held the type of meat that would have gone onto the scrap heap, but Juliette and her mother were grateful nonetheless.

6.

The lessons continued pleasantly enough. Indeed, Juliette despaired of teaching her charge too well and feared the end mind come to her tutoring job. Charles' father continued to take her home in his carriage, always with a stop at the meat market for a few morsels that she could take home for their evening meal. Her mother had begun taking in sewing and was earning a few shillings herself, and she had become quite adept at stretching the meat to cover all seven days of the week. They had really no hopes of improving their situation; they were simply grateful to survive. Juliette tried not to think of her father and how his actions had placed them in this situation. Her mother did the same. It was hard not to love him still.

Charles' father began coming home early to observe their sessions, he said to be sure he was getting his money's worth, but Juliette suspected otherwise. One evening her suspicions were confirmed as Charles was excused from the parlor, but his father made no move to leave, instead encouraging Juliette to sit next to him in front of the fire. The heat of the fire may have been responsible for his suddenly florid complexion, but he hastily stood up behind her and placed his hands on her shoulders. She stiffened but he gradually slid them down to her small breasts. "There, doesn't the fire feel good," he murmured. She too stood up abruptly.

"I must leave. Mum will be worried," Juliette stammered. "I can walk, sir, I don't need the carriage."

"Rubbish. I won't hear of a vulnerable young girl like yourself walking home alone." He threw his cloak on and ushered her out of the parlor. His ardor had not cooled by leaving the fire, however, and once in the coach he drew the curtains and forced himself on Juliette. It was over in minutes. Juliette said nothing and as he departed the coach at the market he roughly handed her a rag. "Clean yourself, girl!" She tugged her dress back into place and did what she could with the rag. When he reentered the coach he handed her a thick parcel which she later discovered contained two plump rib chops, something she hadn't seen since her father was alive.

As soon as Juliette entered their rooms, her mother sensed something was awry, and when she unwrapped the parcel and saw the chops, she knew. She put her arms around Juliette but said nothing. Juliette never shed a tear but set about seasoning the chops while her mother stoked the coals.

Of course the meatpacker's "attentions" continued. He was once even so bold as to assault her in the very parlor of his house, explaining that his wife was at some function or another. Juliette didn't enjoy their encounters, but she thought women were probably subject to worse things such as begging and starving in the streets. She also proved herself a true banker's daughter and the next time the coach stopped in front of the market, she firmly stated, "I'd like some sausages with the chops and perhaps a small roast." The meatpacker was astonished but returned with three wrapped parcels. Juliette knew she had crossed a moral line but put those thoughts aside as she mused about how they might prepare the roast on the weekend.

Not a week later, Juliette and her mother heard the coach draw up outside their rooms, earlier than usual. Juliette grabbed her shawl and her book but was taken aback when she saw the meatpacker's wife at their door. Her imperious look said it all as she took in the shabby little rooms and the pile of sewing on the table. She didn't even glance at Juliette but directed her comments to her mother. "We will no longer require the services of your slatternly daughter," she announced, dropping a shilling on the floor. She swept her coat around her and turned quickly toward the carriage. Juliette was mortified but not nearly so much as her mother. When her mother died several days later, Juliette knew it was from shame. In the coming years she would look back on that experience as she heard many versions of her own story as she moved west: The mister went after me and the missus sent me packing.

7.

It had been four long years since papa's death, Juliette mused as she walked along the waterfront. Although she was only a girl of 16, the experiences of the past few years made her feel like a woman of 40. After her mother's death, Juliette finished the little sewing projects her mother had taken on and collected a few more shillings from her mother's customers. They were only too happy to pay her and shoo her on as, no doubt, her experiences with the meatpacker were well-known among the gossip mongers. Before long she realized she would have to vacate their rooms in the market district and somehow make a new start. She bartered her mother's clothes and even her Bible to one of the market stall vendors in exchange for a sturdy pair of boots, yet she held on to her precious books. Now she looked down at the hard boots she had bargained for and wondered if she would ever see any of the finery she was raised with again.

She had met a young woman in circumstances much like her own during her wanderings on the waterfront and the two agreed to rent a room together. The other girl provided cleaning services to the area businesses, and she hinted, sometimes some other services as well. Shelley encouraged Juliette to join her and oftentimes they worked as a pair. Their earnings were barely enough to keep a roof over their heads but they enjoyed each other's company and felt a bit safer in the rough environs of the shipyards.

Whenever the mostly dank London weather permitted, Juliette would take a book and sit on one of the park benches to read and watch passengers disembarking from one of the grand ships. One such day she watched a gentleman with two small children approach the ticketing booth to inquire about passage to the United States. The children were fussy and kept darting away, once nearly into the path of a carriage and another time scaling the barrier to the water, clearly intent on jumping in. Juliette whistled to catch their attention. "Lads, would you like to be hearing a story?" They turned suddenly shy and hung back near their father, but curiosity won out. Within a few minutes they were seated with Juliette, one on each side of her and quietly listening to her read a story about a king and his castle.

The father concluded his business and turned to look for his boys, clearly astonished to find them quietly sitting with an attractive young girl who appeared to be reading to them. "Say, that's quite the picture," he proclaimed on approaching them. "You've cast a spell for sure. They're never that quiet at home." He doffed his hat and introduced the boys as Arthur and Charles, himself as Mr. Barrett, all the while taking in her worn dress and heavy boots but enthralled by her beautiful auburn curls and blue eyes. When she spoke, he was further amazed, as her accent and demeanor were cultured and clearly educated. Why she could read!

"Thank you sir," Juliette replied with a small curtsy. "They're lovely children, and just being boys you know." He didn't seem to be in a hurry to leave and the boys clamored for another bit of the story. Juliette read for a bit longer while Mr. Barrett leaned against the end of the bench. When she reached the end of the chapter, the king's fate was still uncertain. "Papa, please, can we come back tomorrow to hear more?" Juliette was embarrassed at putting their father in this position, but he was unperturbed.

"I'm sure this young lady has a family of her own to take care of," he assured them while giving her a questioning look.

"Well, no sir, I'm quite alone," she demurred, "and I would be happy to read to the lads again."

He swung his walking stick back and forth and seemed to wrestle with some decision in his mind, finally stating, "Well, then I think here's the solution." She expected he would say the boys could return the next day, or perhaps he would give her their address so she could read to them in their home, but she was unprepared for what followed. "We're leaving in four days hence to sail to the States. I think you should accompany us as a nanny or governess, whatever you'd like to call it." He paused to see her reaction. Seeing her dubious expression, he added, "Of course, I would pay your passage and a little extra. When we get to New York, perhaps we can continue the arrangement there as well."

Juliette was too stunned for words. The States! She had a real opportunity at a new start and nothing would prevent her from taking it, even her fear of being out on the ocean. Finally she collected herself and replied, "Oh, sir, yes, yes, of course." The two discussed the necessary arrangements and Juliette nearly ran back to her room to share the news with Shelley. She was going to the States! She had a job! In the States!

8.

Juliette prayed that she was not about to die. Then the ship lurched over another mountainous wave and she prayed she *would* die. To think that she had to endure two or three more weeks of unending nausea, vomiting and worse was almost too much to bear. Juliette shared a cabin far below-decks with three other women also traveling as nannies. Their accommodations were better than steerage, but they still had no access to a private toilet, having to use a communal bucket which soon overflowed. Everyone drank from barrels of brackish water; fever and dysentery became the norm. The steerage class was responsible for bringing their own food on board, but at least the nannies had some food provided by their employers. The night times were sheer terror as the ship plunged and rolled through the icy Atlantic and everyone below decks suffered in complete darkness. In the morning there would always be two or three dead bodies to be removed and summarily tossed overboard, often to awaiting sharks which followed the ship, adding insult to injury.

During the day the nannies had to somehow straighten and clean themselves before attending to their charges, but at least it gave them time above deck in the open air. Juliette enjoyed the boys and an occasional conversation with Mr. Barrett but she found his wife cold and unwilling to engage in even the smallest pleasantry. Mrs. Barrett looked quite ill herself, and Juliette hoped this alone might account for her general unpleasantness. Juliette found that the motion of the ship made it nearly impossible to read from one of her books without another wave of seasickness, so she and the other nannies resorted to improvising games and contests for the children. They all thought it so comical that there was a cow on deck, specifically to provide fresh milk for the first-class passengers.

With her long curls blowing freely in the ocean breeze, Juliette was a sight to behold, one not lost on the sailors, many of whom attempted to catch her attention and speak with her as she strolled the deck. She would acknowledge none of them, however, as she had already heard tales of what happened to young women preyed upon at night in the pitch-black cabins.

Mrs. Barrett was well aware of the attention Juliette was attracting among the men on the ship, her husband included. They had had a terrible row when he came home from the waterfront that day and announced summarily that he had hired a nanny who would accompany them on the journey and remain in their employ once in New York. Did he think she had no say in the matter of who would attend her children! Then she saw Juliette waiting at the docks and everything became clear. It may be that the harlot was to sail with them to New York, but she vowed that once there, Juliette would be sent packing before her husband could make any further 'arrangements' for her.

On the final morning of the voyage, Juliette heard the steamship horns sounding as she climbed the steps to the deck. Nearly all of the passengers were lining the rails of the ship straining for their first sight of New York City and she hurried to join the Barretts as they did the same. The boys, of course, were trying to climb up on the railing, so Juliette had her hands full restraining them, although finally Mr. Barrett put the younger one on his shoulders for a better view. When Juliette and the older boy found places, their shoulders slumped in a nearly identical manner. They were disappointed in what they saw, a city nowhere near as grand as London and a waterfront just as dirty. Fresh fruits and vegetables were stacked next to steaming piles of horse manure. Carriages lined up for seemingly miles awaiting the disembarking passengers while other wagon drivers jostled for space to unload their goods. It was bedlam with everyone shouting at everyone else, quite unlike the more civilized manners of the English. Juliette was allowed to disembark with the Barretts, ahead of the steerage class, and Mr. Barrett seemed to know exactly which carriage was theirs. The Barretts' luggage would be delivered separately, and of course, Juliette had only her one small bag with a spare dress and her books which she carried with her.

Juliette's spirits were slightly buoyed when they pulled up in front of the townhouse that Mr. Barrett had secured for his family. It was a three-story red brick building with dark green eaves and neatly-trimmed English boxwood shrubs flanking the front entry. Wide gray marble steps led to a double-door entry and beyond that to a high-ceilinged foyer. The parlor and adjacent dining room had silk wall coverings and each room had a fireplace with carved ebony mantelpieces. The boys excitedly ran upstairs searching for their room, or rooms—perhaps each had their own? Juliette waited uneasily in the foyer, not certain which direction she should pursue, while Mr. and Mrs. Barrett adjourned to their own rooms. Finally, a maid came forward and beckoned her to follow. They entered a kitchen at the back of the house rich with food smells, a beef roast, bread baking, the sweet smell of pies. Juliette was nearly overcome with sadness, and hunger, but said nothing. She remembered when her home in London smelled this very same way.

9.

Juliette's happiness was short-lived as the imperious Mrs. Barrett soon came into the kitchen and began giving orders to the maid about when and how to serve the meal. She pointedly told the older woman that "the staff" were not to be served the same food but whatever kitchen scraps remained instead. The maid nodded silently and Juliette saw her hopes of a good meal diminish. Still uncertain as to what to do with herself, Juliette began attempting to help the maid set out serving plates and utensils, but Mrs. Barrett put a stop to that. "Go to your room," and she pointed down a dark flight of stairs behind the kitchen, "and wait until you are called to attend to the children."

The stairs led to a miserable little room even shabbier than those she had endured in London. A lumpy cot that smelled of something rotten was the only piece of furniture in the room. A well-used chamber pot sat underneath it. The depressing dungeon, as Juliette viewed it, was barely lit by a street-level window perhaps the size of two of her books set end-to-end. She supposed she would have to wash up in the kitchen at times when the family was asleep or out of the house. A nail had been driven into the wall, and Juliette used that to hang her bag to keep it away from the mice she was certain would come out at night. She was too tired to even cry about her new home.

The sounds of dinner being served carried down the stairs. After a while Juliette could hear the scraping of chairs being pushed away from the table and she could hear the boys thundering up the stairs to their rooms. Still, no one called for her, but finally the maid did knock at the top of her stairs and set a plate of table scraps down at the top step. The indignity of being fed like a dog was overshadowed by Juliette's hunger; she ate everything on the plate and, not daring to come up to the kitchen, left the plate on the floor. Gradually the house quieted and Juliette could hear the kitchen door close as the maid left for the day. As silently as possible she crept up the stairs hoping to find a pitcher of water to clean herself. She was startled when Mrs. Barrett burst into the kitchen. "What do you think you're doing, girl? Stealing food?" she commanded.

At this, Juliette did burst into tears. "No, ma'am, I was simply hoping for some water to wash myself after this long day." But then she held her head up and added, "I'm an honest person and a clean one!" She turned from Mrs. Barrett and hurried down the stairs, missing the venomous look the mistress of the house cast after her. Juliette slept fitfully and spent the following day awaiting her call to look after the boys; when none came she resigned herself to waiting for her pitiful dinner. Late that night she once again broached the kitchen in search of soap and water. Finding them, she stripped off her dress and stood in her slip, washing first her hair, then moving the soapy rag under her arms, over her breasts and down to her thighs. Mr. Barrett stood watching her in the moonlight, entranced by her long arms and legs and full breasts. A squeak in the floorboards gave his position away and Juliette nearly screamed when she saw him, quickly snatching her dress up in front of her.

"Oh, don't worry dear, I wouldn't touch you," he assured her. "It's just that you're so young and beautiful I couldn't stop myself from watching."

"Well, you shouldn't have," she glared at him. "I don't have a proper room or a decent meal and now I can't even wash myself in private!" He gradually backed out of the kitchen and Juliette quickly finished her ablutions, not wanting to be caught once again by Mrs. Barrett.

But it was Mr. Barrett, in effect, who was caught. When he climbed the stairs to his wife's bedroom and was more attentive than usual, she immediately knew the source of his ardor. She suffered his attentions and then calmly stated, "In the morning you will tell that girl we have no further need of her services." And after a pause, "Do I make myself clear?" He started to protest but knew any further argument would inflame the situation even more. So in the morning, history repeated itself.

Mr. Barrett waited until the boys had left for school then sought out Juliette. "Uh, the boys are in school now so we will no longer be needing your services," he mumbled to her, holding out a few dollar bills. "So, that's it then. There you go." Mrs. Barrett stood in the parlor listening closely to the exchange.

"But, where shall I go?" Juliette cried. "I have no one here in the States." Trying another tack, "And the boys love me, they do." Mr. Barrett was truly sympathetic but could only respond by pressing more money into her hands and indicating that she should collect her belongings while he stood holding open the back kitchen door. He could not meet her eyes as she stepped past him, telling him, "You should be ashamed." He was, but there was nothing to be done about it.

10.

Juliette felt humiliated, angry and frightened. If only her plucky friend Shelley were there to help her! She looked at the money Mr. Barrett had pressed on her and realized she had enough for a night or two at a rooming house, but no more. She started walking toward the waterfront, the only part of town she had seen, dragging her pathetic little bag and avoiding the stares of strangers. When she came to a little park she sat down to rest and think about her choices. Fluttering on one of the benches was an abandoned newspaper, something she hadn't seen in months; they were even hard to come by in London. She passed the afternoon pleasantly reading about events in the world and forgetting for a few moments her own troubles. One column in particular caught her eye describing the goings-on in Virginia City out west. She could hear the piano playing and the laughter of men in a saloon, the train whistle and the pounding of the silver stamping mills in the background. She remembered when she thought she might write about the lively characters of the London waterfront in just such a manner.

But as the sun started to set Juliette realized she would have to find some shelter and also food, so she followed the direction other people seemed to be walking and came upon a marketplace much like the one near where she and her mother had lived. She bought a piece of fruit and ate it ravenously then paid a few pennies for a small loaf of bread. She asked several of the vendors if they knew of rooms to let, but no one had any suggestions. As darkness settled over the market the vendors began to close their stalls and Juliette became quite worried.

A woman a bit older than Juliette had been watching her for some time and finally made her approach. "Alone, are you dearie?" she startled Juliette, touching her shoulder at the same time.

Rightfully suspicious, Juliette replied vaguely, "Well, I'm just looking for rooming houses that might be to my liking." She stood up straight and asked the stranger directly, "You wouldn't know of anything appropriate to a woman like myself, would you?" imagining that she sounded as imperious as the Queen of England.

The woman hid her smile behind a fan, charmed by Juliette's naiveté. "Actually, I do. There are several women such as yourself who share a house together. You would be more than welcome to see if it meets your standards." She waited for a response, then linked her arm through Juliette's and began steering her down the sidewalk, introducing herself as Fran. The neighborhood changed rapidly from the marketplace to a collection of bars and two- or three-story tenements, the residents of which sat on the dirty front steps and watched Fran's and Juliette's progress with great interest. Catcalls emanated from the men, but the women were just as rough in their language and gestures.

Juliette was relieved when Fran lead her through the doors of one of the more gaily-painted rooming houses and surprised to see that the bottom floor was one large open space with several women reclining on couches or sitting at small tables with apparently nothing to do but talk with each other. A central stairway divided the room and as Fran and Juliette made their way inside, a man and woman came down the stairs, laughing and teasing each other. The man tucked a few bills into the woman's bodice and left with a wave to the other girls. She may have been naïve about some things, but Juliette recognized this for what it was. She indignantly pulled away from Fran. "I am not a prostitute, madam, and I use the term purposely," Juliette stated, her blue eyes piercing. Some of the other women chuckled, but a few cast their eyes downward.

"Oh, honey, I didn't think you were," Fran said, endeavoring to slide her arm around Juliette's shoulders. "But you are alone and no doubt penniless, so I was simply offering you our hospitality." She felt Juliette's shoulders sag. "And, if you were to decide…"

Juliette's shoulders went back up and she shrugged off Fran's arm. "I will make no such decision," and then she had a moment's thought, "but I will accept your hospitality for the evening until I make further plans." The evening turned into nearly a week in which Juliette watched how the girls accepted their customers and how little they complained about it. Seeing the dollar bills that even the plainest girl was counting, she made her decision to accept the next customer through the door. Fran smiled and gave her a little encouragement, wryly observing, "What's another slice off a cut loaf?" Juliette was relieved to see the customer was young and as nervous as herself. The whole business was over in minutes and Juliette accepted his two dollars with shaking hands.

In time Juliette learned the little tricks of the trade, how to move the men along faster especially. She insisted that they submit to having their genitals washed before the encounter, and oftentimes the "washing up" was the total act. Even Fran admired her ingenuity.

While Fran was the madam, she also had a boss, a distinguished gentleman who came by the house every week to collect his share of the proceeds. The girls all hoped to catch his eye but he laughed them off and told them he never sampled the merchandise. He was especially excited one day, however, confiding in Fran that he planned to open a house such as this, but grander, in Virginia City, the booming silver town in Nevada. Would she like to go? Could she spare any of the girls? Juliette overheard their conversation and boldly inserted herself. "Sir, I would be honored to be chosen, and I promise you I would work harder than anyone." He could see she was a beauty and her cultured English accent was alluring as well. Fran dismissed her but when the boss came the next week Juliette surprised them both by having her bag packed next to the door; three other girls, at Juliette's urging, had done the same. In days they would be on the train to Virginia City.

11. Jack

Sergeant Jack Bartley had been released from the Richmond garrison a week earlier after two years of fighting for the Union. He was exhausted and still bloody after the last battle near the Kentucky town of Perryville where 7,000 troops perished in only five hours of fighting. His commander, General Don Carlos Buell, praised his men for the victory but Jack thought it was hollow at best. As he trudged along he reflected on all the death and destruction he'd seen in the last two years and thought it was really all for nothing. He, like most Kentucky men, had no real opinion either way on slavery yet was compelled to fight for the Union to bring an end to the practice. Hell, he was lucky to support himself and his wife and daughter, let alone have the money to own a slave and feed him, too.

The thought of reuniting with his wife and seeing his daughter who would now be three years old was what kept him walking nearly day and night to reach home. The army had kept all the horses, which he resented mightily; his horse was deemed vital for the war effort, but he was apparently not, there being no resistance to his leaving at the end of his enlistment. There were many soldiers like himself walking back to their homes, so sometimes Jack had a bit of company, other times not. All of the conversations started the same, "Have you heard…" and then they would ask about the state of their home towns. Jack did the same, asking about his home outside of Bowling Green.

He was astonished to learn from a soldier heading east that Bowling Green had been overtaken by the Confederacy and actually named the capital of the Confederate State of Kentucky. The soldier recalled that occupation probably lasted about a year but said the rebels had been driven out eventually. The news made Jack quicken his step, now fearing how his family might have been affected out on his little farm.

When he was within a few miles of the town he began to see tendrils of black smoke curling up past the trees and his heart began to race. As he crested the hill outside of town his worst fears were confirmed. Bowling Green lay in devastation with hardly a building left standing. As he walked through the destruction he came upon a woman sitting on a burned out log holding a charred tea kettle. Her haunted expression was much like Jack had seen on shell-shocked soldiers after prolonged bloody battles. At this point he prayed that his farm — and his family — had been spared as they were a mile or so out of the path of destruction.

But Jack's prayers were not to be answered that day. The log cabin he had built and the small barn had both burned to the ground; even the corn field was blackened. He stepped gingerly through the wreckage hoping to find some sign that his wife and child had been able to flee the Confederates before their approach. A bundle of rags that might have been a child's doll was off to the side of what was the porch, but otherwise no evidence remained that this was once a family home. He was frantic to think of who might have sheltered his wife and baby but had seen only a few strangers when he came through the town.

As he walked out to the barn to see what, if any, tools remained he came upon the worst discovery. Two graves, one for an adult and one for a child, appeared to have been hastily dug behind the house with dirt mounded up on each less than a foot high. On the graves rested the ultimate desecration— two Confederate uniform buttons. Jack had survived much and witnessed incomparable brutality during this two-year conscription in the Army, but the sight of the two rough graves brought the big man to his knees. He roared in pain and pounded the ground in front of him. He grabbed handfuls of his nearly shoulder length black hair as if to tear it from his head. He ultimately collapsed next to the smaller grave and lay there with his hand on the little mound until darkness set in.

12.

In the days and weeks that followed Jack became a fearsome spectacle. His hair grew longer and his beard more unkempt. He still wore his bloody, tattered uniform although he had lost his cap somewhere along the way. The first few days he had done nothing but collect rocks to place atop the graves to keep scavenging animals at bay. He carved markers for each, "Mary, wife of Jack Bartley, mother to Penny" and "Penny, beloved daughter of Mary and Jack Bartley." Once the graves were properly tended, and still consumed by equal parts rage and sorrow, he stumbled along the road between what was left of the town and the remnants of his homestead.

He had taken to drinking at the only remaining saloon and stayed long into the night daring anyone to stop him. Many mornings found him passed out along the road or in an alleyway behind the saloon. He refused to speak to anyone, especially other former soldiers, and if anyone tried too aggressively to reach him he more often than not would beat them to a bloody pulp, his hands like anvils, some said.

On one such evening there was a stranger at the bar who watched Jack stare morosely into his whiskey, the now half-empty bottle a testament to his state of mind. One of the local men attempted to josh him just a bit. "Say, fella, war's about over. Whyn't you get out of that old uniform, become a farmer again?" The man never knew what hit him. Jack lunged out of the chair, grabbed the man's shirt front and hit him hard enough with one punch that he was unconscious before he hit the floor.

"Anyone else got a problem with this uniform?" he bellowed. "Maybe some of you was wearin' the other color, heh?" The remaining patrons steadfastly went back to their own drinks and no one dared reply. No one but the stranger, at least. He approached Jack's table with a fresh bottle of whiskey, gingerly setting it down in front of Jack. "I don't need nobody buying me a drink," Jack growled. "Leave me to it!"

"Well, sir, I'm not so much buying you a drink as proposin' to share one with you," the stranger replied, standing his ground. "Eugene T. Matthews at your service," he said with a flourish, extending his hand to Jack.

Reluctantly shaking the proffered hand, Jack kicked back the extra chair at his table and motioned for Matthews to sit. "And what service would that be?" Jack asked guardedly.

"Why to make you rich!" Then, lowering his voice and leaning toward Jack, he continued cautiously. "I've seen those fists in action, my boy. I know what all's happened to your family," and at this Jack bristled but Matthews continued, "so I know you're angry and have a right to be, but let's do something with that anger." The thought hung in the air between them.

Finally, Jack asked, "What do I got to do? Kill people for you?"

"No, no, no, my boy," Matthews countered, warming to the discussion. "Why I'd like you to box for me, put on exhibitions and the like." Growing more enthusiastic, he added, "We would travel to the county fairs and festivals and so on."

Jack looked skeptical. "Don't you think people has had enough with fighting, with the war and all?"

"Sadly, I suppose not. Of course, a lot of them never saw it first-hand and close-up like you did," he reassured Jack. "No, I think there's plenty that would pay to see a real first-class boxing exhibition." At the mention of pay, Jack seemed more interested, so Matthews pressed the point. "We'd split the gate, 50/50, you and me, and I'd pay your expenses." He slapped Jack on the back. "It'd be grand, my boy, just grand."

Jack finished off his already open bottle of whiskey and they started on the second. After Matthews described the train and riverboat traveling they would enjoy and the adventures they would have, Jack's shoulders finally slumped in acceptance. "Well, I guess I can just as easy starve there as starve here," and the deal was struck. From that day forward he would be known as Black Jack Bartley, master of the ring and taker of all challengers.

13.

Matthews had a very well done-up wagon pulled by a lively set of matching bays. In the back was an assortment of flags and banners proclaiming, "A Night of Pugilistic Perfection," or others that said, "A Fine Fare of Fisticuffs." Matthews would always enter a town with flare, trotting briskly the length of the town and back before stopping in the middle to tie up the horses and unfurl a few of the banners. Then he and Jack would begin a leisurely stroll through the streets with Matthews doffing his hat at every lady and shaking hands with most of the men. "Eugene T. Matthews, at your service, and this is here is Black Jack Bartley, the finest boxer ever to grace our state." He had by now outfitted Jack in a new Union uniform, although in truth he was no longer a soldier. "Don't matter a bit," he reassured Jack. "People like to see a soldier like yourself who come out just fine."

When townsfolk would ask about the banners, Matthews would point to Jack proudly. "This young man has fists of iron and the speed of a cougar, and for a small wager he'll take on any of you in the ring." Then slyly, "He ain't been beat yet, but there's always a first time for everything…" After a perfunctory stop in to see the town sheriff about staging the event, he and Jack would continue their stroll. But resentment flared from time to time. "I ain't no trained pony you can just lead around," Jack lashed out, although, in fact, he realized that's exactly what he was.

He thought back to their first day on the road. They had traveled about 10 miles from Bowling Green to another even smaller hamlet and Matthews went through his usual routine. A surprisingly good crowd of about 50 men and a few boys, no ladies, lined the sides of a makeshift boxing ring in a farmer's field just at the edge of town. Three local farmers, all younger than Jack, had signed up with Matthews for the chance to beat Jack and win a purse as great as $20 (or so Matthews promised). Jack stood sullenly in one corner watching Matthews collect the admission and lay down the bets. The farmers were clearly nervous but excited, frequently slapping each other on the backs and sticking their chests out. Everyone seemed grateful for the diversion from the daily challenge of rebuilding their farms and their town.

Finally, Matthews rang a rusty old bell to settle everyone down. "Welcome, welcome gents and lads to a night that will not disappoint," he bowed with a flourish. "Our journey here has been most pleasant and we are eager to put on a good show for you all." A smattering of applause arose and got much louder when Matthews introduced the first contender, a slow-footed boy of about 18 who was cheered on by three younger brothers, all with tousled blonde hair and pink complexions. The hard work of clearing forested land and putting in crops hadn't seemed to have hardened their bodies much at all. A few jeers greeted the introduction of Black Jack Bartley, but when Jack removed his uniform jacket to show a chest and back of rippling hard muscles, the jeering died off.

Matthews explained the rules of the fight, three rounds, clean fighting, no hitting below the belt, and a white towel thrown into the ring signals stopping the fight, by either side. The bell rang to begin the first round and the farmer danced toward where Jack stood waiting, flat-footed. The boy had the confidence of the untested but he was a moment too slow in putting up his fists to protect his face. Jack hit him once and down he went. His brothers were so shocked they waited nearly 30 seconds to drag his limp body from the ring. The second contender stepped into the ring, showing a chest and arms of sinewy muscle. Head held high and fists up he approached Jack more slowly, feinting with a left hook and then a right jab. Jack maintained his position until the challenger took one step closer too many whereupon Jack felled him with a mighty right. This time his friends dragged him from the ring more quickly. It appeared that the third challenger of the night was having his doubts, but his friends pressed him into the ring and Matthews once again rang the rusty bell. It was over in less than a minute. Jack put his jacket back on and strode from the ring, although Matthews was trying in vain to hold up Jack's fist in victory.

In the rooming house that night, Matthews tried to coach Jack. "You just need a little finesse, my boy, give 'em a little show."

Jack glared back. "I won, didn't I? You got paid, didn't you?" At this last question Matthews looked a little uneasy, wondering if Jack had seen him pocket the extra two dollars.

"Well, yes, we both got paid," Matthews persisted, "but we could have worked them up to betting more, you know, stretched out the fights a bit, made it look fair."

A deep laugh coming from Jack surprised Matthews entirely. "Fair, what's fair?" he questioned. "Having a battle-hardened soldier beat the hell out of some farmers who never saw it coming?" After more pleading on the part of Matthews, Jack allowed that he would try to put some 'sport' in it next time.

14.

The beating was vicious. He could feel ribs breaking on both sides of his chest, he spit up two teeth and was amazed his head was still on his neck. He looked toward his corner, imploring him to throw down the white flag and end the carnage, but Matthews looked away and let Jack be beaten to a bloody pulp for the full third round. When it was finally over, his opponent walked up to where he lay and extended a hand to help him to his feet. The crowd had been booing the victor for all three rounds, but it hadn't slowed him down. Now, he helped Jack gingerly to his feet. "No hard feelings, I hope, mister," he quietly explained. "It's just that even here in the North it's hard for a black man to get a start." Jack grimaced but said nothing as his opponent continued. "I got a piece of land and a little family, so I need some money to get some seed, maybe a cow…" he trailed off.

Jack nodded and put his hand on the man's shoulder. "I respect that," and after a moment, "sir. We're all doing what we need to get by." Jack shuffled to the edge of the ring, holding onto the ropes and winced when he climbed out. Matthews started to slap him on the back but thought better of it just in time.

"Well, son, it happens, it happens," he said nervously. "But, we took in about double what we've made in those other towns."

"We?" Jack asked incredulously. "*We* didn't lose teeth. *We* won't be laid up with broken ribs for God knows how long, will *we*?"

Matthews knew when to silently agree, which he did now, thinking it was a good time to change the subject. "So, my boy, when we get to the Mississippi we're faced with a decision." He helped Jack lie down in the back of the wagon and continued, "Should we head south from St. Louis, hit Perryville, Memphis, Baton Rouge?" His enthusiasm increased. "Why, we could go over to New Orleans, meet some of them saucy Southern gals! Rest up a bit, go fishin', whatever you want, really." At the mention of Perryville Jack stiffened, although Matthews thought it was just a reaction to pain from his ribs as the wagon hit a pothole. Jack said nothing but he thought back to that terrible battle and he considered what going into the South would mean for him. He knew he'd see his wife's and his daughter's murderer in every Southern face he saw. Jack was no philosopher but he knew it would be adding coals to the fire of his rage and ultimately consume him entirely. "I think we best go north," he finally groaned out. Then, knowing what drove Matthews' thinking, "Folks up north probably got a bit more money."

"True, true," Matthews said thoughtfully. "Plus, I suppose some old boy would take a pot shot at you if'n you entered the ring in your old uniform." He actually laughed. Jack just closed his eyes and endured the rest of the ride in silence. For the next several days Jack lay in the wagon as they passed through small towns, although he rallied enough for the crossing of the Ohio River on a small ferry. He began insisting that they stop at a saloon in every town, however, telling Matthews, "I think some whiskey would relax these ribs, help me heal up." Matthews was doubtful but wanted to keep Jack satisfied for the time being, so most evenings found them in a small town saloon.

One such night in the small town of Anna in southern Illinois, Matthews drifted through the saloon chatting up the locals about what passed for entertainment in these parts. One old man volunteered, "Well, we had us the circus here a few weeks back. Everybody enjoyed it greatly, I suppose." He began to laugh, "We especially liked that dancing bear! Damnedst thing you ever saw." He went on to describe a brown bear "tall as man" when standing on its hind legs. He slapped his thigh and went on, "Lordy, I tell you when they put a straw hat and a little skirt on it and let it dance to a polka, there weren't a person in the tent that wasn't laughin' their head plain off."

Matthews was suddenly interested, "So, that circus has moved on, has it?" he asked the old-timer.

"Oh, yeah, they folded up their tents and went on toward St. Louie I reckon." Then he laughed some more. "But that old bear, he didn't move on with them."

"Oh, and why not?" Matthews inquired quite seriously.

"I reckon it cost a bit to feed him and the circus folks thought they could just hire a clown as cheap," the old man ruminated. "Course, I don't think it'd be as funny, an old clown, you know?"

Matthews bought the codger a whiskey and returned to the table with Jack. Ever the entrepreneur, Matthews began thinking. Why, dancing could be made to look like fighting! Wouldn't that be something! He envisioned a new set of banners showing a daunting grizzly facing the bare-chested soldier, towering over him with teeth bared. It would bring the crowds in for sure! The next day while Jack slept off the night's whiskey, Matthews set out to find the farmer currently housing the bear. After a very short negotiation, the bear was loaded into the back of Matthews' wagon, rather docilely, he observed, and the two returned to town to collect Jack (who would now have to ride on the wagon seat, of course).

Jack fairly exploded when he saw their new traveling companion. "You want me to do what?" he yelled at Matthews. "I ain't getting in the ring with no wild animal! I ain't doin' it." Matthews pointed out that he wasn't really all that wild, look how nice he sits in the back of the wagon. The three rode on in silence for the next two days, but even Jack couldn't help but notice how passersby reacted to seeing a bear in the back of their wagon. He allowed that it could help bring in the crowds, a boxing bear. He finally gave in and at the next town Matthews had the new banners printed up.

15.

Traveling with the bear in tow had meant they couldn't stay at a hotel or a rooming house, of course, so they resorted to sleeping in the back of the wagon while the bear was tied to an axle. The bear made the horses a little skittish, but nothing seemed to bother the bear, Jack noticed. In fact, when they fed him he just sat and ate quite companionably. One day Jack decided to leave his chain untethered, but the bear made no move to leave their little campsite, and Jack realized it was because he had become so domesticated, probably starting as a cub, that he felt no inclination to flee to the woods.

Matthews rode one of the horses into town to get the banners while Jack stayed behind with the bear. He tried to rile the bear up a bit, to no avail, and Jack began to think this new venture of a boxing bear would be a colossal failure. When Matthews rode back into their camp with the new banners, he was clearly pleased with how they had turned out, and he said he had another idea, too. "I think, my boy, we should take a stick or some such and give you some scratches on your back and sides, you know, like bear scratches." Jack looked at him dumbly. "It makes it look like you and the bear have already done a few rough rounds," Matthews explained while searching for a sharp stick.

"You come near me with that stick and I'll turn the bear loose on you!" Jack threatened. Matthews dropped the stick but persisted with the idea, suggesting perhaps they could tear Jack's shirt or his pants just a bit, but Jack gave him a cold glare that kept Matthews away.

The next day they rode into another little hamlet just south of St. Louis and Matthews made his usual circuit of the main street, letting people see the bear in the back of the wagon, then made a second loop to set out the banners. For this night's event Jack would take on two challengers and then, assuming he survived, would fight the fearsome giant grizzly as the finale. As Matthews predicted, the event drew the biggest crowd yet. Jack handily put down the challengers, leaving a bit of their pride intact by suffering a few light blows himself before ending the bouts with his lethal right hook. And then it was time for the bear to enter the ring.

Showman that he was, Matthews had procured a length of chain that took two men to carry to lead the bear into the ring, although Jack knew he would have just ambled in on his own quite readily. "Ladies and gentlemen," Matthews intoned. "He's fought the rebels in many a gruesome battle and came out without a scratch." And then building the excitement, "Why he's fought some of the toughest men this side of the Mississippi." Lowering his voice just slightly, "Has he lost to any of them?" Some in the crowd yelled back, "No, no." But Matthews pressed on. "He only lost once, but even that opponent was well bloodied by the third round and vowed never to enter a ring again." At this, Jack tried to look a little sheepish. "But, ladies and gentlemen, tonight Black Jack Bartley faces a challenger unlike any other for the very first time right here in your town." He gestured toward the bear, hoping for a growl, but the bear simply put up a paw and waved. The crowd chuckled, a bit nervously perhaps. Judging that he had drawn the event out long enough, Matthews finally rang the old bell.

Jack approached the bear with his fists held high. The bear reared up on its hind legs and the crowd gasped. It was easily as tall as Jack, perhaps an inch or two taller even. It walked toward Jack and put both paws on Jack's shoulders. If the fight had ended in a knock-out it would have been because of the bear's breath. Jack nearly fainted at the smell of it. It wasn't in him to punch the bear, but he pushed him back roughly. No scratch marks remained because the bear's claws had long ago been cut and filed down. The bear stood on all fours, then reared back up and approached Jack again. This time he looked into the bear's eyes and realized how old he was and that he was doing as he was trained to do; the bear just wanted to dance. Jack didn't let him get quite within reach, backing up slowly and turning slightly to the right as he went. Then in a burst of speed no one would have expected from the big man, Jack spun around and came up behind the bear. With his long arms, he reached around the grizzly and pinned the bear's front legs to his chest. At this the bear did growl, which urged the crowd to whistle and stamp their feet.

Surprising the crowd and himself, Jack pulled the bear back toward him until the bear was off balance and starting to lose his footing. With one massive heave, Jack leaned back and brought the bear to rest on the ground between his own legs. He clamped his legs over the bear's and the two rocked back and forth like children on a swing. The crowd went wild with laughter and dollar bills and coins were passed to the stage. Jack kept a firm grip on the docile bear, feigning a huge effort with a grimly determined look on his face. Matthews kept his distance from the bear but declared Jack the winner, collected the money, and called for the ring boys to bring out the huge chain to secure the bear.

When the field had emptied out and the townsfolk departed, Jack told Matthews. "That old bear's got no more fight in him than you do. I ain't getting' in the ring with him again." Matthews sputtered and held up the bucket full of money, but Jack was steadfast. He quietly went out to where the bear was tethered and quickly put him out of his misery. It was no way for a proud animal to live; it was as demeaning to the bear as it was to Jack.

Matthews wasn't happy but said nothing and the next day they rode into St. Louis where Matthews bought them two tickets on a riverboat steamship heading north.

16.

Jack loved the steamship travel and spent all day and most nights out on the deck watching the countryside drift by. Matthews stayed in his cabin scheming up their next entertainment program or prowling the deck hunting up a poker game. They were headed for St. Louis, the second largest port in the country, New York City being the only one larger. Their journey would take more than a week, but it was still much faster than plodding along in a wagon. Matthews had made a pretty penny on his wagon and the matched bays, but it meant he had to give up most of his banners and flags. Of course, those depicting the bear would have been useless anyway.

The boat stopped frequently to pick up more wood for the massive steam engines and to load other sundry supplies and travelers. Jack enjoyed standing by the rail watching all the activity. The further north they journeyed, the fewer soldiers Jack saw, which suited him just fine. He longed to put the war and everything associated with it behind him. The rhythmic churning of the paddlewheel soothed him like no whiskey ever had.

Matthews met every group of new arrivals with his usual flourish, introducing himself as a poker player of modest skill. "Perhaps once you're settled in, gents, we'll break out the cards?" he queried of any likely looking rubes. Many of the communities along the river had banned gambling houses, but no such regulation existed on the river where hundreds of boats each day made their way up and down the grand Mississippi. Matthews was in favor of changing boats at every reasonably sized port and hoped to enlist Jack in resuming his boxing career in wharfside matches, but Jack was having none of it, nor would he participate in matches on board.

"I believe my fighting days are over," he proclaimed one morning. "I'm sure you'll think of some other enterprise we can get up to," he teased his partner. Matthews was in no mood for even the gentlest teasing. As Jack became more relaxed, Matthews became more restive and the partnership became strained to the point where a day might elapse in which they didn't speak to each other at all. Jack realized something else one sunny afternoon. The feelings of rage and sorrow he had been carrying over the loss of his family were softening into something entirely different. He now felt comforted that he had enjoyed the love of a good woman and from that a beautiful little girl. He spent the afternoon musing over the moments they had shared rather than mourning the ones they would never see.

Jack supposed he and Matthews would part ways in St. Louis, but he had made up his mind to head further west. He was a better poker player than he had ever let on to Matthews so he supposed he could pick up a few dollars on the way. Matthews had grown tired of the riverboat life and half imagined he might get off in St. Louis and try to find that traveling circus, the one that had left behind the old bear. He could be an advance man, of sorts, staying a town or so ahead of the circus and promoting its arrival. Perhaps eventually he could be the ringmaster. He had the sales skills, by God!

But a sort of inertia overtook both men and after a day or two of gambling (and a little whoring) in St. Louis they decided to sail a bit further north together. The next big stop was Hannibal, Missouri, a town that sorely tempted Jack to put down roots. From the deck he could see virtually every kind of tree—maple, ash, hickory, dogwood, oak, black gum and sassafras dotted the river bluffs in a profusion of color. Jack envisioned clearing a small space of land, as he had done in Bowling Green, building a small cabin and then sitting out on the porch in the afternoon to watch the changing of the seasons. He knew from fellow passengers that Hannibal had attracted all sorts of immigrants and had been welcoming to them all. Vast slaughterhouses could be seen a distance from the river with thousands of cattle and pigs waiting in pens. The downtown seemed to have all the businesses anyone would need.

As their steamboat pulled away from shore, Jack and Matthews heard another familiar sound, a train whistle. Jack had been on his share of trains while serving in the army and had no particular desire to board another, but Matthews soon convinced him that opportunity lay to the west. They hurried to the station for tickets and caught the train as it was leaving Hannibal to journey all the way across the state to the end of the line in St. Joseph. Start-up towns with curious names like Shelbina, Laclede, Chillicothe and Hemple all looked about the same. Jack and Matthews drifted along companionably, wondering whether they would proceed even further west or turn back to the security of an established city like Hannibal or even St. Louis.

As the train moved further through Missouri, the would-be farmers and their families disembarked, ultimately leaving men who talked of nothing but staking a claim in the mining boom of the Nevada territory. By the time St. Joseph came into view, both men had caught the fever as well. Wagon companies were lined up at the train station promising a safe passage to the West. Matthews talked their fares down as far as possible while Jack shopped for whatever provisions the two might need on the trip. They were likely to be crossing the plains and the formidable mountains beyond them for months, and although the Indian wars had died down this far north, Jack figured on buying plenty of ammunition especially.

17. Padraig

If he lived to be 50, and he crossed himself at this, he'd never forget the haunted look on his ma's face as she begged along the roadside, the two tiny girls clinging to her skirts while he and his older sister foraged in the nearby field for any leftover potatoes. Her humiliation, fear and sorrow were written large and she had long ago given up any pretense of encouraging the children that everything would work out fine. He, too, had stopped trying to make a game for his little sisters out of finding food. Padraig had been five years old when the blight struck the potatoes in his father's field and all those around them. He couldn't remember having a full belly since then. Now, five years later his mother was reduced to making soup out of dirt and twigs they gathered. She herself was so weak she could barely stand at the road. Padraig scoffed and told her he didn't know why she even tried begging—there was no food to buy anyway.

They had stayed in their single-room mud cabin in a cluster of other such meager dwellings. The groupings, or clachans, at least gave them some protection from the landlord's middlemen who might try to evict them in the middle of the night or from others who would try to take advantage of them in other ways. Normally they would have had a pig and a few chickens sharing the clachans but those had long since been sold.

In the evening the residents used to enjoy sitting together, singing, telling jokes and recounting the day's events. Now they just huddled miserably. The main topic of conversation was the blight, of course, and speculation on what had caused it. The only thing the farmers had to eat in this part of the country was potatoes, and even as a boy Padraig could eat pounds of them—or at least he used to be able to. Potatoes were planted around St. Patrick's day and harvested in late September or October, so there some lean months up close to harvest time, but nothing like this. Many agreed that the blight which turned the potatoes black and inedible, leaving an incredible stench, might be a plague from God. Indeed, the Protestants in England claimed just such a thing, that the Catholics brought it on themselves by being lazy. Padraig only knew that his father and the other men in the clachan had worked hard, just as he expected to, and he did not know why God would single them out for such misery.

Many of them, including Padraig's father, John Kelly, had left their families behind to go to England and work on the harvest, hoping to earn enough money to feed their families. However, what they did earn was barely enough to feed themselves and they came home to their emaciated families with empty pockets. They also told chilling tales of seeing shallow mass graves alongside the roads and huts that were burned to the ground with the now-dead residents inside. Padraig's father said he heard a speech while in England that claimed as many as a million Irish would be dead by next year. Another million would try to escape by fleeing to England, Canada and even America. Padraig couldn't imagine leaving his family, but the thought of going to America did spark something in his imagination.

Finally, with no other alternative short of starving to death, Padraig's father announced that the family would report to one of the workhouses in nearby County Galway. The workhouses were a creation of the British but each was supervised by a Master and a Matron, the whole affair being supervised by the Poor Law Commissioner in Dublin. Padraig's ma and sisters cried when they heard and insisted they could try to make it through just one more winter, but John Kelly was adamant. He would not see more of his children die in the cold with their bellies protruding and their limbs just sticks.

The first thing Kelly and Padraig, now a strapping lad of 12, would lose at the workhouse was their pride. On arriving the man of the household was questioned, in front of everyone, about why he had no way of providing for his family. Kelly held his head high but softly admitted, "It's the potatoes. Sir. There's no way of getting any with the blight, and there is nothing to eat." He stuck his chin out, "I and my son here would do any job you'd give us to put food on our table, but there ain't none of those either, beggin' your pardon." The gavel came down and they were accepted, joining another thousand or so other Irish families, but then they had a second thing to lose. Families were separated as men and boys went to dormitories away from the women and girls. The indignities piled up. The families had their clothes removed and were washed down crudely, then given rough cotton uniforms. From that point forward they were forbidden to leave the workhouse, except for the men who were sent out to break stones to build new roadways. Women were kept busy knitting while the older girls were trained in factory-type jobs and the younger drilled in school lessons. The dreary atmosphere was made more so by the rules against talking during mealtimes. There was no time for the family to be together except during Sunday church service.

Kelly felt his family probably resented his choice, but Padraig could see what it had cost his old man and he was determined to hide any shame from him. When the blight came to an end, and when he was older, and when his family moved back, and when and when; his thoughts swirled around all day and night in a poignant torture.

18.

After six long years, the potato blight finally ended. The workhouses were closed and the families in them reunited but uncertain as to where they would go next. Would their former landlords allow them back to the little plots they had tended before? Padraig's family faced this worry and more. Ma had died a year into their stay at the workhouse, probably from shame, Padraig thought. His father had become a shell of the robust, hearty man he once was. Now, it would fall to Padraig, 16 years old, to be the man of the family and look out for his three sisters, two younger, one older than himself. Having had only the brief Sunday meetings with each other in the workhouse, they were virtual strangers but Padraig felt the responsibility for them weigh heavily.

His father led them back to their original home in the neighboring county. They passed numerous gravesites along the way but found their own camp much as they had left it. The girls set to cleaning up the little mud hut while Padraig and his father began digging trenches in which to plant the few seed potatoes they had been given. How they would survive from the planting to the harvest some six months later was something Padraig couldn't contemplate, throwing himself feverishly into working the field and helping the other members of the clachan who drifted back.

His sisters solved part of his problem for him. The eldest announced that she would go to Dublin and find work as a seamstress there, something she had been trained for in the workhouse; she knew other young women like herself who had made similar plans. The two youngest had come much under the influence of the nuns in the workhouse and proclaimed their intentions to take the vows and become nuns, journeying to a convent in County Cork where the nuns would be expecting them. Padraig and his father watched them leave, but there were few tears on either side. They had been through terrifyingly difficult times and survived, so this was just another step. Many Irish families had suffered worse indeed.

"You know son," his father began one day as they put aside their tools, "you don't want to be just livin' and workin' for nothin' but potatoes your whole life, like I did." Padraig began to protest that it had been a good life before the famine, but his father stopped him. "I'm telling you that you're a fine lad, smart and strong, and you should have a better life. You need to go to America and just leave your old pa here with the potatoes." Padraig was shocked but also knew it was something he had been thinking about ever since they entered the workhouse.

"I don't know as how I could just leave you, pa," he said softly.

"I'm nearly 40, not long for this life, I expect." The silence between the two stretched on until finally he clapped his hand on Padraig's shoulder and said, "Well, it's settled then. We'll get this crop out of the ground, maybe sell some of it and get some money together for a ticket on one of the ships to America." They spent the rest of the evening discussing what each had heard about America and the opportunities there, excitement tempered with sadness. In the coming months Padraig worked hard on their own plot and also hired himself out to others to do any job available.

His father went back to the road-building job he had before the famine. Now, hundreds of thousands of men, women and children were put to work building stone roads throughout rural Ireland. It was make-work but it was hard work. Men hammered stones into smaller pieces that could be carried by the women in baskets. Children helped fit the pieces into place. All were paid by the piece. The pay was so poor that the workers could scarcely feed themselves. John Kelly ultimately was one of the workers who simply collapsed with his hammer in his hand. Padraig buried the hammer with him. Not long after, the work projects were suspended and replaced with soup kitchens to help feed the starving nation. It was the ultimate indignity for Padraig and he vowed to be first in line for a ship out of Cork harbor to America.

19.

Padraig became well-acquainted with Cork Harbor. While he waited for the potato harvest time he went to the harbor and picked up occasional jobs unloading ships. Although the blight seemed a thing of the past, the upcoming harvest was months off and would not yield the potatoes needed to feed the farmers and provide seed potatoes for the next year. In response, the government imported huge shipments of corn and grain supposedly designed to fend off starvation. Instead, workers like Padraig ferried the shipments past starving people to warehouses where the grains remained, moldering because no one could afford to buy them.

While working in the harbor, Padraig learned of two possible routes to America. He had seen poor families evicted from their cottages and then placed onto ships to America with the promise of food, a little money and jobs awaiting them. Others found "sponsors" who offered the same enticements and said that once the families arrived they would be met by agents, fellow Irishmen indeed, who would help them get settled. Padraig never did hear how these arrangements worked out, as none of the poor ever returned, but it stayed in the back of his mind.

The decision was made for him as soon as he had completed the harvest. An eviction notice was nailed to his cottage door giving him a day to vacate the property or face arrest. Carrying the largest sack of potatoes he could manage and wearing both of the shirts he owned, plus his father's old jacket, he made his way to the harbor and was immediately met by one of the sponsors. "Say, you're a strappin' big lad," the man addressed Padraig, "just the kind of worker they're looking for in America."

Padraig didn't know whether to believe the man or not and felt he had little choice but to follow him to a rickety-looking sailing ship gradually filling up with passengers who looked much like himself, ragged and worn down. They would travel below-decks in steerage and it was clear they were to provide their own food for the journey which could last anywhere from one to three months depending on the weather. Some 300 passengers were crammed into the dark space with only a few sleeping racks and no privacy. Padraig and the others jockeyed for floor space, hopefully away from the slop buckets.

"You know what they're callin' these boats, don't ye?" an elderly man asked Padraig as the ship left the harbor. "They're callin' 'em coffin ships, they are." Padraig nodded but chose not to continue the conversation. He knew children were listening and didn't want to scare them or, in fact, voice his own fears. The very first night at sea proved a harbinger for the journey. At least one woman wailed all night and many others cried. Padraig fought to keep down the vision of his mother and sisters in the rolling, stinking black hell that was steerage class. As he thought of them, he hoped that his sisters' commitment to the church had at least given his mother's soul some peace.

Every morning the sailors would open the hatches and allow some fresh sea air into the hold. The slop buckets were passed upward and buckets of water passed back down. Only on rare occasions were the Irish allowed to leave the hold, and then it was usually to attend the burial at sea of one of their family members who had passed on in the night. Everyone was infested with lice, Padraig included, and with the lice came typhus which easily devastated the weakened, malnourished emigrants. Padraig had survived cholera in the workhouse and hoped he would fight off the typhus as well, but every day was a struggle for survival and sanity.

After nearly a month at sea Padraig was surprised to learn that their ship would be going to Canada, not America, but at that point nothing mattered to the passengers but getting off the ship and onto steady dry land. When at last the ship entered the Saint Lawrence River after a 3,000-mile journey, the passengers expected to be let off immediately; instead they sat for days and days in quarantine, becoming, in fact, sicker by the day.

Padraig tried to help with children, devising games for them to play to give their weary mothers some respite, and his efforts attracted the attention of a young woman close to his own age, probably 16 or so, with flaming red hair that she had cut short at the start of the voyage, despairing of any way to keep it clean and lice-free. Padraig had no experience around women other than his sisters, so his attempts at conversation were awkward, but she seemed to welcome it.

"I'm Padraig Kelly," he said as he proffered his hand to her. "I'm traveling by myself to America."

She laughed, "Well, actually you're traveling with 300 of us to Canada."

He blushed and then laughed along with her. "And you? Your folks are on board?"

She cast her eyes down and said softly, "My ma died the first week out, then one of my brothers, so it's just my father and me," and she pointed in the direction of a gaunt man lying near the bottom of the stairs. Padraig had been watching the man for the last several days and doubted he would get off the ship alive. "Where's me manners!" She put her hand out to Padraig. "I'm Kathleen Finegan of Kildare." Her hand was tiny in his and at that moment he vowed to himself that he would protect her. He also said a prayer to his mother, thanking her for sending an angel to guide his way to America.

20.

After weeks of waiting to be examined, the passengers were unceremoniously dumped off the ship and told to make their way to a hospital to be released from the quarantine or treated. Some were so weak that they died along the roadside, one such person being Kathleen's father. Padraig stacked his body with several others while Kathleen said a prayer and clutched her rosary. It was an awful end to the old man's journey after suffering through the ocean crossing, but there was nothing to be done.

"I think if we go to the hospital, we'll just be waiting again with people much sicker than ourselves," Padraig told Kathleen. "I think it would be best if we just kept moving," and he hesitated, "that is, if you're throwin' your lot in with mine."

"And some lot it is," she smiled through her tears. "If you say that's what we'll do, then I guess we better just do it." She took one last look back at her father and took Padraig's hand. They walked away from the hospital and toward a village they could see in the distance, hoping to find other Irish settled there who would take them in at least temporarily. They found the village anything but welcoming, and as soon as it was obvious they were Irish, they were turned away everywhere, the locals being afraid of catching typhus. Padraig and Kathleen spent the first night off the ship huddled and freezing in the Canadian woods, trying to reassure each other that tomorrow would be better. It wasn't. In addition to the locals' fear of typhus, they faced a strong anti-Catholic sentiment and were simply pointed down the road leading across the border to America.

They trudged along with other Irish they met along the way, all with similar tales to share. In the Irish tradition, at least they pooled their meager resources and made their way across the border. Many expected that if they could get to New York they would meet the "sponsors" that had been promised them when they left Ireland; Padraig had begun to doubt there was any such thing, but already he had learned much about survival. In upstate New York their little group was met by "runners" sent out to recruit the Irish, even speaking to them in Gaelic, promising to help find them housing and work. The housing turned out to be filthy, crowded tenements, but as Kathleen reassured Padraig, "At least we're not dying by the roadside." The dying did continue, however; six out of ten Irish children born in America didn't see their sixth birthday, and the adult Irish lived only about six years after arriving in America.

Padraig and the other men accepted the lowest-paying, most back-breaking jobs and returned to the squalor at night. Kathleen contributed a few dollars by taking in laundry from the single men in their cramped building, and somehow the couple managed to get by. Padraig steadfastly refused to give in to the nightly rituals of whiskey-drinking in their tenement. "It's the curse of the Irish," he told the other men. He personally believed the drinking and lying about just reinforced the anti-Irish sentiment that was so common, that and the Irishmen's willingness to accept almost any wage. Soon, signs began appearing, "No Irish Need Apply." Padraig tried to make light of it, singing as he walked down the sidewalk, "Oh, NINA, my NINA, where are ya' when I need ya?" He was almost happy his father wasn't with him to see the conditions they lived in and the open hostility and hatred they faced.

When Padraig stumbled over a drunken young girl—she couldn't have been more than ten--lying in the tenement entrance one evening, he turned away in shame, telling Kathleen later, "We can't stay in this place. It's not safe for you." He confessed, "It's not safe for my pride either," adding, "and that's part of what keeps me going." She understood and repeated her willingness to follow him wherever he thought was best. A few days later he announced that he had signed on to dig canals out in western Pennsylvania and that they would be leaving within the week.

Padraig and others toiled on the canal-building, and when the ground got too frozen to sink a pick into, he signed up to work on a railroad line pushing west. He had always lived in close proximity to other Irish families, enjoying the daily conversations and especially the ever-present joking and teasing, but the more he saw of the wide-open country that lay before him, the more he felt drawn to the west, and Kathleen said she felt it, too. "Ah, when you look at that big sky, you just want to stretch your arms up and grab it all," she said and twirled around. Her luxurious red hair had grown back by now and Padraig was enthralled by her beauty and his good fortune in having found her.

"I just want to stretch out and grab *you*," he laughed, chasing her around in front of their house. The railroad had provided some basic housing for the workers; the cabins were actually dismantled and moved a few miles as the railroad progressed. They could be reassembled just as easily. Padraig's only discontentment came from working for a wage and being told what to do every day. He remembered that even potato farming had given him a little individual freedom and he longed for that feeling again. It was only natural then, that when he met other Irish who had captured the dreams of being gold and silver miners, staking their own claims, that Padraig would yearn to go as well. When the railroad reached its end point for the season, Padraig vowed to go on; he and Kathleen got tickets on a wagon train heading west.

21.

"You ever worked deep underground, boy?" the mine superintendent asked Philip. The other miners began to laugh out loud, goading the superintendent. "Ah, you can see he's afraid of the dark," or "I suppose his mama tucked him in and left a candle burning all night." The bantering went on until Philip was red in the face and clenching his fists. The superintendent told the other miners to get back to work and told Philip to sit down and calm down. "This kind of work ain't for everyone," he started. "It's dangerous, it's hot, you're all cramped up down there, and swinging a pick for eight hours is damn hard work."

"I'm used to hard work, sir," Philip leaned forward eagerly. "I helped my family build a farm out of nothin' but dust and dirt, and we had a house, too."

The super had recognized a former Great Plains farmer the minute he saw Philip, but he had to admit it was strong of the boy to control his temper with the other miners and be straightforward about his background. He decided to give him a chance. "It's two dollars a day and you start tomorrow, sharp at 6 a.m." He saw Philip's eager grin and became more stern with him. "You get yourself some sturdy boots and gloves, we'll give you the rest. That's it then, go on with you." He stood up and motioned toward the door.

"You won't be sorry, sir. I'll work hard as any man out there," Philip said defiantly. Only in town two days and he already had a job! It was going to work out just fine. Unfortunately that feeling lasted until the noon whistle the next day. The pick was heavier than any he had ever used to break up dirt clods on the farm. He wasn't used to working bent over by almost half. The pitch-black darkness was unsettling and the noises the rocks made sounded like the whole mountain was about to cave in on them. It was hot in the mine and difficult to breathe. Riding out of the tunnel on the little ore cars was the best part of the day.

The other miners had little to say to Philip other than to admonish him to look before he swung the pick back lest he gore one of his neighbors. Most of them were Cornish or Irish since the tin mines in Cornwall, England, were much the same with their square-set timbers, pumps and drills. Philip was astounded to see the deep natural hot springs in the mines, as arid as the land around Virginia City appeared, but no matter how many pumps were placed the miners were still standing in knee-deep hot water for much of the day. He survived his first day and collapsed on returning to the rooming house where most of the other boarders were miners, too. If one of the others hadn't roused him in the morning, he believed he would have slept through the entire next day. But, he put his heavy boots on and trudged to the mine entrance with the others.

The next day was exactly the same although word spread that one of the tributary tunnels had collapsed, trapping and killing perhaps a half-dozen men. There was a moment of silence among the men working next to Philip, some crossed themselves and said a prayer, but then it was back to work. Philip broke up rocks that the others had broken off the tunnel walls, but he never did recognize the silver-blue metal that had caused all the excitement in the first place. One of the old hands told him, "They was gold miners here before and they all complained about this sludge that fouled up the gold sluices." He laughed and spit a mouthful of tobacco. "Wasn't for a while that somebody realized that nasty stuff was silver, and here we are today." He could see Philip's eyes light up at the mention of the gold but quickly added, "Gold's all played out now, so don't be hopin' you'll find yourself a big old nugget."

The first week crawled by but at the end of the shift on Saturday, he did agree to go to the saloon with some of the men, flush with their pay and eager for a pint of beer or a shot or two of whiskey. There were over a hundred saloons to choose from, but the miner's favorite was the Delta in the center of town on C. Street. Philip and his new friends found a table and they quickly filled him in on the local lore about how one mine owner supposedly lost $70,000 playing poker in one night, then shot and killed himself right at the table. It happened with two other gamblers, they asserted, and now the roped-off table in the back was known as the Suicide Table. Philip shuddered at the story but also marveled that anyone could have $70,000 to gamble away. He had seven dollars in his pocket and it was the most money he'd ever had.

22.

Philip learned that the mine he had been working in had reached a depth of 3,000 feet, which astounded him when he realized it was the better part of a mile deep; no wonder it was also nearly 100 degrees in the deep tunnels. He was too inexperienced to be sent to that depth (and much relieved to learn so) and remained at the intermediary levels breaking up rocks and loading the ore carts. He'd grown used to the constant pounding noises from the stamping mills that ran all day and all night long, refining the silver to be sent by rail down to the mint in Carson City. While he was happy to collect his pay each week, he had to admit to himself that he could not stay in the mines. He believed he was destined for a better life, although he wouldn't admit it to anyone out loud.

At the end of another back-breaking week when he and the men ventured into the Delta, Philip got his beer and walked over to a neglected piano that had been pushed off to the side next to the Suicide Table. Dust and grime coated the keys but when Philip played a few notes, it was reasonably in tune, at least as much as any of the drinking miners would discern. He pulled up a chair and began to play a few of the songs he had entertained the regulars with in the bar on the Plains. Matthews and Jack were in the Delta having a few whiskeys, and when Matthews heard the hearty applause Philip drew with his first few songs, the hustler launched into action.

"Eugene T. Matthews at your service," he said, approaching Philip with a fresh beer. "I believe I can judge talent when I see it, my boy," and he leaned in conspiratorially, "and I believe I see it in you."

Jack watched in amusement as Matthews probed the boy's background and asked what his present "means of employment" might be. Philip was flattered but wary of the flamboyant Matthews and gave guarded answers, saying only that he was "in the mines" and had been taught the piano by his mother who was "elsewheres." Matthews was undaunted, however, and plied Philip with another beer, encouraging him to play a few more songs for the gents.

"Now, that was fine, my boy," he said after a little waltz number, "but you see, we're not in a church here, we're in a saloon. The music's got to be lively, lively so the men will feel like drinking." He could see Philip was offended and tried to soften the blow. "But it's grand, just grand to find someone with your talent out in such a rough area." He assured Philip he would see him again and perhaps talk about promoting him into some more "reputable" venues.

Jack had gone back to musing about their trip west. He had enjoyed it immensely and felt his soul become more at peace with every mile. Their wagon driver was an old hand, experienced with avoiding the occasional roving bands of Sioux Indians, so Jack could have saved the money he spent on ammunition. The wide-open country enthralled him. "There's a lot of it out there, ain't there," he remarked to Matthews nearly every day. When they neared Virginia City they spotted a herd of wild horses, mustangs, the wagon driver told Jack. "You can't tame 'em for anything, but they're a joy to see, all right." Jack couldn't have agreed more and reckoned he would buy a horse when they got to Virginia City just so he could ride out to the hills and watch for them.

Jack's reverie was broken by the sound of a chair crashing to the floor and glasses breaking. Two of the miners were throwing wild punches and causing more damage to the saloon than to each other. When they got a little too close to Jack, he stepped up and grabbed both of them by the backs of their shirts, handily dragging them to the saloon doors and pushing them out into the street where they could continue their mayhem unimpeded. The bartender and waitresses were already in the process of cleaning up when Jack came back into the saloon. The bartender waved him over, gesturing with a fresh beer. "So, that was quick thinking, mister. Otherwise, they would've tore up half the place."

Jack accepted the beer and said, "Oh, they're just lettin' off steam. I reckon working down in those old tunnels could make a man half crazy." The two watched the barmaids right the tables and clean up what large pieces of glass they could.

Finally, the bartender broke the silence. "You know, they're looking for a bartender over at the Bucket of Blood, and I could put a word in there for you."

Jack realized he couldn't continue living off the largesse of Matthews forever. They had been passing the time playing dominoes every afternoon while Matthews badgered Jack about returning to the ring. In fact, he told Jack one such lazy afternoon, there was a world-class prize fighter training right here in Virginia City for a big match down the hill in Carson City. Jack could be his sparring partner, Matthews reasoned, and maybe get a spot for himself on the fight card.

Jack looked at the bartender and thought about his choices. "I reckon I'd be a good barkeep. I'm no stranger to a bottle of whiskey, for sure, and I think I can keep the peace all right," Jack promised, laying his big hands on the bar. The next day found Jack sauntering into the notorious Bucket of Blood saloon, a step down from the Delta perhaps, but not the worst saloon in town by a long shot.

23.

The wagon trip had been a tedious time for all involved, although the closer they got to the Nevada Territory, even the girls perked up a bit. Juliette had tried to make the long days a little more interesting by reading to the girls and the handful of other passengers in their wagon and encouraging them to make up stories of their own about the "wild West." Inevitably, the whores' stories circled around to the same wishful dream.

The girls would giggle and tell stories of whores they knew who had become kept, or even married. "I knew a whore once in Boston whose regular customer turned out to be a Senator, and he set her up in one of the fanciest houses in the city," one would say. Another girl heard of the same thing happening in New York City where she had worked previously. "And you shoulda seen the clothes she wore!" After such a story-telling session the girls would look off across the vast land and sigh…it could happen to them. Why not?

At 17 Juliette hardly felt prepared to be anyone's mother, but that was what she had become to the other whores on the wagon. Their hard exteriors hid fragile, frightened young women who found any hope tenuous. They looked to Juliette for guidance and reassurance and were clearly in awe of the fact that she could read so easily and eloquently. Of course, they had asked her, "Why you? Why are you a whore?"

All she could reply was, "Circumstances happen, but we make the best of them." And then with great seriousness, she looked at each of them. "What we do is not who we are." She repeated it, "What we *do* is not who we *are*." She encouraged them to freshen up and hold their heads up high.

They knew that word of a fresh shipment of whores coming to Virginia City had already reached the town. The faster stage-coach drivers were the biggest source of gossip and news, and they had encountered several on their slower wagon journey. The first few days in town would likely be exhausting, Juliette agreed, but in a backhanded way reassured them that their novelty would wear off before long. One of the whores was a black girl who kept mostly to herself, and Juliette wondered about her fate. Would she be prized as exotic or scorned as nothing more than an ex-slave (if indeed that's what she was)?

Although Juliette tried to keep things interesting, it was the wagon master who provided the most entertainment. Early in the trip he approached Juliette about having a free "romp." After all, he told her, "I'm protecting you from Indians, why saving your life is what I'm doing," and he got quite indignant. He was an old man with two sets of suspenders on to hold his pants up under the weight of a prodigious belly. The seat of his pants was shiny from all the time spent on the wagon bench. His full beard most often showcased the last meal. In short, he was quite an unattractive man. However, some nights he did play the fiddle and knew a few jokes that were appropriate for the whole group, although he laughed the loudest, a braying sound that upset the horses.

Juliette grew pensive at his proposal. "Well, I suppose I would have to calculate the cost of this romp, as you put it," and she pretended to count on her fingers. "Would it just be me, or each of us?"

"Oh, well, you first," he said, quite flustered, "you being the prettiest and all." He hesitated a moment, "But the others, too, of course."

Ever the banker's daughter, she went back to her 'calculations' and said, "Well, at two dollars a romp with six whores," and here she stopped. "Now, how often? Every day? Off on Sunday?"

"Every day?" He recovered enough to state boldly, "I suppose every day might be enough."

"Hmmm, six days a week, six whores, two dollars a romp, that's 12 dollars a week," Juliette stated, "and, of course, I would need an extra four dollars to administer the whole thing, so 16 dollars a week." She knew she had him. "If you were short a few dollars, I'm sure when we get to Virginia City I could talk to your company about your arrangement with your paying passengers and they'd make up the difference."

"My company!" He was so flustered that his chewing tobacco dribbled completely out of his mouth and into his beard. "Well, I don't think that's necessary."

"So, you have the 16 dollars now?" Juliette persisted.

He allowed that he didn't but persisted in saying he deserved a free romp for all the protecting them against Indians that he was doing.

"But, sir, you don't have any Indians either," Juliette announced with finality. The other whores listening to the negotiation broke into raucous laughter at this point and the wagon master stomped off to attend to the horses. From that day forward the girls teased him all the more outrageously. At the end of the journey he was sheepish and said he would miss them like daughters.

One couple that stayed away from the whores and out of most of the discussions was Padraig and Kathleen. This suited Juliette just fine; being English, of course, she had no regard for the Irish. What she saw of them in New York had convinced her they were nothing but lazy drunks and petty thieves whose wives were driven to exhaustion caring for large broods of sniveling children.

A few nights before they reached Virginia City, however, Kathleen approached Juliette. "What do you suppose this city will be like?" she inquired.

"I expect it will be pretty rough," Juliette said thoughtfully. "After all, mining is dirty hard work and with the town being so new I don't expect anyone's had much time to fancy it up." She pointed to their fellow passengers and added, out of their earshot, "I guess with these kind of newcomers, it won't be much." She expected Kathleen to cry, perhaps, but she was surprised.

"Well, I suppose you're right, but then that means just more opportunity, too."

"Is your husband going into the mines, then?" Juliette had observed that Kathleen and Padraig kept their distance from each other. "Or brother?"

"I guess it's nothing to a whore," Kathleen huffed. "We're just traveling together is all." And then she thought to add, "We come over on the boat together and my pa and brother died, so Padraig kind of looked after me."

"Well, how nice of him," Juliette simpered. "And I'm sure he'll just keep doing that for nothin'…" Now she could see Kathleen brimming with tears. "Oh, honey, maybe he's just waitin' till he gets some money put aside to ask you to marry him."

"I hadn't thought that," Kathleen replied, looking a little less tearful. "I supposed I'd be takin' care of myself once we got to the city."

Juliette was learning to look at everything as an opportunity. She leaned forward and brushed the girl's luxurious red hair out of her face. "Ever think about becoming a whore?"

24.

The moment Juliette posed her question to Kathleen, she felt Padraig's presence behind her. "I won't have you talkin' to a lady such as Miss Finegan about whoring!" he angrily announced, at the same time taking Kathleen's arm and roughly pulling her off the log where they had been sitting. Kathleen was partly shocked and angered but also pleased that he was still her protector. Still…

"I will talk to whoever I please," she informed Padraig, "whenever and wherever, and I'll thank you to unhand me." She stomped away from him and climbed up, unassisted, into the wagon. They were only a day's travel outside of Virginia City, but it was a long day indeed as neither said another word to the other. As the wagon pulled slowly up the eastern slope of Mt. Davidson, Virginia City came into view and finally the silence was broken.

"It's a bit bigger than I thought," Kathleen exclaimed.

"Yes, it's a lively-looking place," Padraig agreed, and then taking her hand, he pointed to a church steeple prominent in the center of town. "And that's where I'll be marrying you, Sunday next," and hesitating a little, added, "that's if you'll still have me and the priest ain't too busy."

"Well, I don't suppose the priest will be too busy to save me from becoming a whore!" She couldn't resist teasing him, but he clearly didn't think it was something to jest about.

"Now, you just stop with that talk." He put his arm around her shoulder and lowered his voice. "You'll always be a lady, and I'll always respect and treat you like one." She leaned her head on his shoulder and the question was obviously settled.

Theirs was one of a long line of wagons entering the city and observed by a well-dressed group of men in The Corner Saloon, the nicest in town situated as it was adjoining the famous Piper's Opera House. "Look at that, will you? There must be 300 people just in those wagons alone," observed William Sharon, the banker. His fellow banker, William Ralston, agreed, tipping his cigar ash into the crystal ashtray provided.

"Yes, and every one of them looking to get rich quick." He watched the men and a few women clamber down from the wagons and collect their meager belongings. "I wonder how many of them will be here a year from now?"

John Mackay, who started as a miner and was now a mine owner, overheard the conversation. "They'll be here till the silver runs out," but he laughed. "That means they'll be here till they're old enough for the cemetery, gentlemen. That silver vein is so big we'll never see the end of it." The men clinked their glasses in salute, but each ruminated on whether Mackay's boast was correct and what it would mean for them if it weren't. Sharon, Ralston and the other "bank crowd," as they were called, were sending the milled silver by the railcar to San Francisco where they had established the stock market, built banks and invested heavily in real estate. They bragged that the city by the Bay wouldn't exist without Virginia City's riches, and they were correct.

San Francisco had its charms, of course, and when the railcars came back to Virginia City they were laden with the finest food, wine, furnishings and the like that the Comstock millionaires had come to enjoy. Even Mackay and his hardscrabble miner partner John Fair had built mansions in Virginia City and entertained lavishly. The city of 25,000 was becoming one of the most powerful financial engines in the country.

Of course, most of the newcomers to Virginia City never experienced the rarified atmosphere of The Corner Saloon.

Juliette and the other girls had been met at the depot by the man who had financed their trip west, Bill Wynn, and another woman in her 30s who he introduced simply as Flo. It was Flo who would show them the ropes, as it were, and he admonished them. "What Flo says you do is what you do, no questions asked." They were loaded into another wagon and virtually paraded down C. Street. Miners hooted and doffed their hats, calling out that they would see the girls later. Juliette had no doubt that there would be lines waiting that night and for several nights in the near future.

She had thought they would be going to a large house like the one where she had worked in New York City, but instead the wagon stopped at what could only be described as a tent camp and what she later learned was called The Line. She sunk up to her ankles in mud when she alighted from the wagon, and she noticed that Flo wore man's boots, not the dainty slippers she would have expected from the madam. The girls were assigned tents, two girls to a tent with just a sheet for a partition down the middle. The tents had wooden sides up to about waist-high and were a scant two feet from each other. Each had two cots, a small washstand and a tiny closet. The floors had boards here and there but were mostly dirt. There was a row of outhouses out back.

"Well, ain't this the Ritz?" Juliette's tent-mate remarked. "I wonder where I'll keep my furs?"

Juliette laughed wryly but said simply, "Well, we made our choice and there's no going back now, is there?" She supposed the work would be the same whether she was in a mansion or a mud hut. Flo came by and interrupted their laughter, calling all the girls to a meeting in her own tent, which was actually not much nicer. Men were already lining up outside, so Flo said she would make the meeting short and let the girls get on with it.

"Everybody pays first," she began. "That's the number one rule. No exceptions, and if I find out you've been giving it away, you'll be out in the street." The girls nodded silently and Flo continued. "You do what they ask you to do, but let them know that if it's out of the ordinary, they're going to pay more for it, and," she paused, and Juliette and others said in unison, "And pay first." She told the girls that Chinese porters would be bringing in hot water and towels, which relieved Juliette greatly. They would work every day and were expected to line up in front of their tents for the miners to make their choice. Hence, the name, The Line, Juliette learned. Juliette expected to be one of the more popular choices with her dark auburn curls and flashing blue eyes. She was correct and the next few days were a nightmare.

Kathleen, meanwhile, was stepping into a nightmare of her own.

25.

The first thing Padraig had done on their arrival was to inquire about the Irish section, knowing they would congregate just as they had in the old country. The wagon master shook his head and pointed to a collection of shacks and tents near the stamping mill. The horrific noise of the mill could be heard throughout the city but in the Irish shanty town it was nearly unbearable as every few seconds ore was crushed so that the silver could be extracted. Of course, the powerful steam motor to run the mill was every bit as loud. Even the roughest times in Ireland hadn't prepared Kathleen for the Irish section of Virginia City, a slum rivaling any in the larger cities.

Padraig introduced himself to a collection of men sitting on a sagging porch, and after a brief discussion it was discovered that he had a cousin, John, named after his own father, who worked in the mines and lived a few doors down. Padraig took this as another good sign although Kathleen was uncertain as they trudged along in the dirt and dust.

Scruffy-looking children were everywhere, seemingly free to do as they chose as no one seemed to be watching them, Kathleen noted. When they reached the door to John's house, Padraig knocked loudly and waited. Hearing children crying inside the house, Kathleen suggested that maybe they should come back later when John was sure to be home from the mines, but the door was opened by a spent-looking young woman who eyed them warily.

"I'm Padraig Kelly, cousin to John, and this is Kathleen Finegan of Kildare." The woman opened the door another few inches but was hardly welcoming.

"I don't suppose John knew you were coming?" she said, hanging onto the door frame while two children peeked out behind her.

"No, that's a fact," Padraig said, "and I didn't know he was here, either, but still…" He didn't know what else to say to the woman, but Kathleen solved the stalemate.

"We've been traveling for weeks and perhaps you could tell us where we could wait for your husband to come home." She stood up straight and added, "We wouldn't want to inconvenience you any, of course."

The woman knew she had been rude to keep them standing on the porch and finally showed them into the two-room shack. "He'll be along any time," she said, "ifn he don't stop at the bar on the way home, and then," she trailed off, "who knows." She finally had them sit at the crude dining table and gave them water but didn't seem inclined to any more conversation. Padraig and Kathleen waited awkwardly until the door was finally flung open by a ruddy-faced, dust-covered man.

"Say, Paddy! I heard a rascal cousin of mine had come to darken our door," he laughed and hugged Padraig vigorously. After introductions were made John insisted that they stay with them until they could find proper housing. His wife looked appalled but said nothing. John pulled Padraig aside and asked, "So, she's not your wife? What the…"

Padraig rushed to reassure him. "Oh, we're getting married just as soon as the priest can get it done. We met on the boat coming over and she lost her pa, so we just, you know, traveled together." He knew he was blushing and what the statement implied, but he also knew John wouldn't believe the truth of the matter.

After a sparse dinner and with John reassuring Padraig that he would take him to the mines in the morning and certainly get him a job, it was determined that Kathleen would share the bed with his wife and the children while John and Padraig slept on the floor. Kathleen had never felt so uncomfortable and vowed to find another arrangement first thing in the morning. There had to be some sort of a boarding house.

The stamping mill ran all night and Kathleen couldn't imagine how anyone got any sleep. It may have explained why the children were so fussy in the morning. Truly it seemed like every Irish child in Virginia City was crying the next morning when she arose. The men left early and Kathleen helped John's wife tidy up a bit, then announced she was going out to see what sort of arrangements could be made.

She ignored the bold stares of the men lingering in the street as she made her way back to C. Street, the main street in the city. She knew Padraig would be angry to learn she had gone out on her own, but John's meek little wife was certainly no help. Idly she wondered how Juliette was faring, but of course, she would never venture to find out. She tramped around the city for most of the day but finally had to return to the Irish section in defeat. She had found no place for a single woman to board although she had received plenty of rude suggestions on the matter.

Padraig came home with John that night, and true to his word, John had gotten him a job in the mill that same day. After a while, he assured Padraig, he would be taken down into the mines, a more dangerous but slightly better paying job. John would also put the word out that they needed a house, but only after Padraig and Kathleen married. The couple spent several more grim nights with Padraig's cousin, but when Sunday came around they all went to St. Theresa's Church of the Mountains. After the service, Padraig and Kathleen met with the parish priest who said he could perform the service the following Sunday. He also knew of a couple who were "in the family way" and therefore moving to a larger house, so he felt certain Padraig and Kathleen could move right after the wedding.

So, a week later Kathleen found herself in a borrowed wedding dress that had been let out and taken in for so many different brides that it was almost more thread than cloth. She was, however, a beautiful bride with her lustrous red hair and emerald-green eyes; Padraig was bursting with pride as he stood by the altar. A few of the families threw a little wedding luncheon for them afterwards and followed them to the shack that would be their new home, providing a few hand-me-downs that would at least get them started. Kathleen knew she should be happier, but something pulled at her spirit. That night in the narrow little bed, the marriage began with a fumbling consummation that left her feeling even more hopeless. She knew preventing a baby was a sin, but she prayed vigorously that one would not result.

26.

Padraig was well-liked by the men in the mines and quickly progressed from the dusty mill work to working in the tunnels. He enjoyed the joking that was second-nature to the Irish and, although the work was hard, he felt the pay was good. He was shocked then when Kathleen announced her intention to find some work, sewing, cleaning, whatever. "I can't spend one more day sittin' in this house by myself," she declared. When he suggested she visit with the other Irish housewives, she laughed ruefully, "What, so I can look after their snotty-nosed brats?"

He was becoming well aware of her Irish temper, so just patted her hand, and hoping to reassure her, suggested, "Well, you'll be a mother yourself soon enough." She glared at him and thought to herself, "Not if the Lord hears my prayers." When he left for the mine the next day, she went back up to C. Street determined to find work but decided this time she would go a block or two above C. Street to the finer homes and businesses where, if people rejected her, at least they might do it in a more kindly fashion, although she knew the anti-Irish sentiment was strong here, too.

As she passed the opera house, she head the most lovely melody being played on a piano. A side door was propped open to catch the breeze, and Kathleen let herself sit on the edge of the wooden steps to listen for a bit. Between the music and the warm sunshine, she must have fallen asleep for a minute or two and was awakened by someone gently shaking her shoulder. A heavy-set lady of about 40 stood there with a pincushion in hand. "Dearie, you can't be sittin' here. The orchestra will be coming in soon and they'll trample you right over."

Kathleen was embarrassed but recovered quickly. "Oh, I'm so sorry. I just heard the music and it was ever so lovely." Unexpectedly tears filled her eyes. "It's been so long since I've heard anything but that mill," and she pointed down the hill.

"Oh, I know what you're sayin," the lady said, patting her on the arm. "Come in then, if you will, and have a cup of tea with me." Kathleen started to refuse but realized it was the first kindness she had been shown. When they went in the building the lady led Kathleen to a small room off the stage that was filled with theatrical costumes and scraps of fabric everywhere. Seeing her questioning look, she told Kathleen. "I'm the wardrobe mistress, make all the costumes I do."

"Oh, I love to sew," Kathleen said earnestly. "I don't suppose you could use an assistant, or someone to clean up after you?"

"Well, tell the truth, it's not much work since they only do but one or two plays a season, so it's just freshening up and little repairs." She could see Kathleen's disappointment but offered, "Still, you could come by in the afternoons, visit with me and, who knows?" She pulled a stack of fabric off a chair and motioned Kathleen to sit. "Now, tell me your name and where you're from." The two talked for the rest of the afternoon, Kathleen unburdening herself of her doubts about her marriage and how she would survive in Virginia City.

The orchestra began arriving for rehearsal and Kathleen realized she might have over-stayed her welcome. "Let me help you take these jackets out to the stage," she said eagerly. The older woman piled Kathleen's arms high with velvet jackets and motioned her out to the stage where the orchestra was setting up. In her haste to be helpful, however, Kathleen knocked over one of the music stands, sending sheet music flying. The piano player watched her and started to come to her aid. Kathleen was apologizing profusely to the violinist and gathering up the music, looking at each sheet and carefully putting them back in order.

"So, you read music, do you?" he asked.

She was embarrassed nearly to the point of tears but composed herself, "My father played the violin and I spent hours listening to him and learning the music." She felt things couldn't possibly go any worse so plunged ahead with her question. "What was the tune you were playing earlier? I couldn't tear myself away from listening to it."

"Oh, just a little waltz that I wrote myself." Now it was his turn to blush. "It's not very good but kind of you to say you enjoyed it." He extended his hand. "Philip Finch. I play here part-time and at the Delta." And then he realized no young lady would be familiar with the Delta. "The Delta is a saloon, no place you'd ever go."

"Kathleen Finegan," she said, taking his hand, "I mean Kelly."

"Kelly Finegan?" he teased her. "I think Kathleen suits you better."

The wardrobe mistress watched the exchange from the side of the stage and thought it might be well if she rescued her new friend before things went any further. "*Mrs.* Kelly, will you come gather this drapery material with me?"

Kathleen hastened to help her then said she best be getting home to start dinner, although lately Padraig had been spending more and more time at the bars and missing dinner entirely. Today Kathleen didn't care at all. She had made a new friend, maybe two friends, and she had heard music, something she hadn't realized how much she missed!

27.

It didn't take Flo long to see that Juliette would be much better working the brothel attached to the Delta than standing in the mud on The Line; doing so would also bring in more money for everyone, of course. She came to Juliette early one morning and told her to collect her few belongings, her books, of course, a hairbrush and a couple of dresses. At first Juliette became indignant that she was about to be thrown out to the street, but Flo reassured her. "Ah, you're too much of a star to hide your light." The madam called for a carriage to be brought round and bundled Juliette into it. They traveled the few blocks to the back entrance of the Delta on B. Street and she led Juliette up the stairs.

Here, each girl had her own room fitted out with a brass bed, chamber pot, wash stand, closet and mirror, plus a pretty little dressing stand. It wasn't what Juliette had grown up with as a girl, but it was so much better than anywhere else she had been in so many years that she was moved to hug Flo. "Oh, I won't disappoint you and Mr. Wynn," she assured her. The procedures were all the same except that the money would be collected downstairs in the saloon before anyone came up to the girls' rooms. The girls were to stay on the railing overlooking the saloon so the customers could make their choice. It beat standing in the mud outside their tents!

That night Juliette took extra care with her curls and her dress, wanting to make her 'debut' something memorable. By now Jack had moved from the Bucket of Blood to the Delta and when he came through the saloon doors at the start of his shift, he felt his heart nearly stop when he glanced up at the railing. It was his wife's ghost. The new girl everyone had been talking about was the picture of what his wife had looked like when they married. He didn't see how he could possibly work and look at her, and when the first man of the evening selected her, Jack thought he might be sick.

Soon, the saloon began to fill up and on this night in particular, the E. Clampus Vitus group took center stage to host an initiation of a new member. The club members were recognizable by their red shirts and black hats, and drinking was a big part of their tradition. Tonight was Sean McNulty's turn to prove his loyalty to the "widders and orphans" of miners; all he had to do was bite the head off a live chicken. He held the chicken tightly under one arm and with a twinkle in his eye, asked, "Might I have a pinch of salt with this hen?" Then without further hesitation he bit off the chicken's head, then dropped the chicken which staggered for a few steps, blood spurting from its neck. When at last the chicken collapsed, McNulty grabbed it and tucked it back under his arm. "I guess I'll be takin' this home to the missus for a fine Sunday dinner." The saloon exploded with laughter, the other miners pounding the tables to the point of nearly tipping over their beers. Bowing grandly, McNulty left the saloon with his prize. He would be a Clamper for life and be wearing the red shirt at the next meeting.

Padraig was among those enjoying the hilarity, his cousin John having stood him to a few beers again. He had been drunk nearly every night and was ashamed of himself; this wasn't the kind of man he was nor the reason he had come to America. He was more ashamed of how he treated Kathleen when he staggered home on these nights to find her sitting sullenly in front of a cold pot of food. He had taken to hitting her, something he saw his father do to his mother and vowed he would never repeat…but he had. When John slapped another beer down in front of him, he put it out of his mind, however.

The mood was anything but frivolous in the private back room of the Corner Saloon at Piper's Opera House. The mine and mill owners were meeting with the bankers and the discussion had been heated about how to attract more East Coast investors to bring much-needed money to expand the Silver Lode. The new style of mining, needing massive amounts of timber that had to be hauled from the Sierras by train and even by log flume; the extra rail cars to transport the ore to the mills; the expensive milling equipment itself, all these things added up and the millionaires in the room weren't about to see their share of the profits decline by footing the whole bill themselves. They knew from frequent visits to the East coast cities that Virginia City and the Nevada Territory in general were regarded as some half-civilized outpost that would suffer the boom-and-bust cycle of the California Gold Rush. James Fair, the miner, and William Ralston, the banker, agreed on one thing: Nevada needed to become a State to gain the respect—and the money—of the Easterners. Gradually, Ralston, with his patrician accent and stiff black suit, convinced the others to begin drafting a constitution and to approach President Lincoln directly with their desire for statehood.

Fair, a much cruder man from the rough-and-tumble days of working in the mines, made the case more directly. "He needs us worse than we need him," he said of Lincoln. "He knows he ain't gonna be elected again and he ain't gonna to have a snowball's chance in hell of getting the slavery ban passed unless he gets our votes." As he sat, the others nodded thoughtfully and it was agreed over a round of brandies that the task of writing the constitution would be done and done quickly. A week later, it was done, and to prove their urgent desire, every word was sent by telegraph to Washington, D. C., at a staggering cost of $3,416.77. Nevada became a state in 1864, President Lincoln was re-elected and the 13th Amendment to the Constitution, banning slavery, was enacted.

28.

The things men would confess to a whore amazed and delighted Juliette. Although some of her customers were just there to get the deed done, most seemed to want to talk to her a bit and relax in her comfortable room for a few extra minutes. With her by-now-standard washing up ritual, often the talk was all they got, she mused. Still, Juliette did her best not to embarrass them, cooing, "Oh, don't be upset. It has been a long time, hasn't it?" Their anger, embarrassment or frustration would seep away as she spent a few moments just talking with them about what tunnels they were working, had any more of their relatives arrived from the old sod, and so on. And, when she walked them back down to the saloon, she always made a point out of appearing to fix her hair and straighten her dress, looking for all the world like the deed had been done and done well.

The best part of Juliette's day was in the early afternoon. She would go down to the saloon and sit looking out the front window onto the hustle and bustle of C. Street. If Jack the bartender were on duty, they always managed to exchange a few words, too. Unwittingly, he was also contributing to her secret passion. Juliette had begun writing a weekly column, "The Tattler's Tale," for the newspaper, The Territorial Enterprise, in which she shared some of the tidbits gleaned from her customers, anonymously, of course. Sometimes Jack would add just the detail she needed as she innocently inquired of him, "So, it's Mr. Gilbert that owns the dry goods store?" He'd answer and stare at her moon-eyed, something she was well used to. He wondered to himself, "Did anyone ever marry a whore?"

The editor who was by now gaining almost celebrity status even on the East coast, encouraged her enthusiastically but was frustrated because he couldn't write a column about the "Purple Prose Prostitute," or some other silly title without giving away her identity. Samuel Clemens told her quite seriously, "Miss, I don't have to edit your work a whit. You're a natural writer and someday..." but they both knew she would never be any more than she was now. Still she enjoyed sharing her little secrets. "Which high society lady slipped while alighting from a carriage at the Sharon House, sliding all the way down the icy hill on her arse, across Front Street, skirts billowing and silk bloomers on display, finally coming to a stop in a snow bank in front of St. Theresa's Church? Such a string of cursing won't likely be heard for some months to come." And the Tattler continued, "Her male escort for the evening was too overcome with laughter to be of any assistance although he did dispatch the carriage driver to collect the woman and deliver her home to dry bloomers." Another column asked the question, "Is a well-known mercantile man setting up a love nest on Third Street for a favorite lady of the night? Did his wife unknowingly help pick out the rose pattern wall paper?" It was all Juliette could do not to preen when she heard her customers talk about that week's Tattler.

Kathleen and the wardrobe mistress often shared a cup of tea while reading the Tattler, and one day the wardrobe mistress found just the opportunity she had been looking for with Kathleen. She knew Kathleen came to Piper's as much to see Philip as to help her with the costumes, and she was afraid where their innocent conversations might lead. "Can you just imagine how angry a husband might be if he found out his wife were consorting with another man?"

"Oh, bother," Kathleen said. "She was probably 'consorting' because he didn't pay her any attention, unless it was with the back of his hand." The wardrobe mistress had seen Kathleen's bruises from time to time and knew she was speaking of herself.

"Still, it's all innocent until it ain't," the mistress said, looking Kathleen directly in the eye. "Men don't have the same responsibilities as women. You know that." Kathleen said nothing so the older woman continued. "It's all well and good for men to take up with other women, sometimes even when they're married. People just say, 'well, he's a man.' But when a woman does it," and this time she took Kathleen's hand, "it can end badly, very badly indeed." She set Kathleen to ironing the orchestra's shirts but could see she was just listening for the first few notes of the piano.

29.

In fact, the Tattler had heard about "a certain piano player who might be tickling more than the ivories," but Juliette wouldn't write the story; she felt sorry for her old wagon-mate Kathleen, seeing her occasionally as she trudged back down the hill from the opera house to the Irish shanties. She also saw Padraig in the saloon from time to time, although never upstairs, largely due to finances, not fidelity, she suspected. Even when she had to service a grunting, sweating, stinking miner who reminded her of a pig rutting, she reminded herself, things could be worse.

Things could not get any worse for Jack, however. He made up his mind that he had to leave the Delta. He simply couldn't watch Juliette lead another man up those stairs; it was like burying his wife a dozen times over each night. He was pleased to see Philip, the Delta's former piano player, come in one such evening and immediately set up a shot for him.

"Still pouring that rot-gut, are you," Philip scowled, although he immediately downed the shot and set the glass up for another.

"Oh, I suppose all you drink now is champagne and French brandy," Jack mocked him. "And how is it we common folk are graced by your presence this fine evening?" he said with a bow.

"Actually, my good man, I've come to rescue you from this den of iniquity," Philip said quite seriously. "It seems that certain parties at The Corner Saloon have come to notice you and wonder if perhaps you would consider joining our fine establishment." He took in Jack's look of astonishment and quickly added, laughing, "Unless, of course, they've already made you part owner here?"

Jack ignored a customer tapping his beer mug on the bar. "You're not just having some fun with me are you?" He pulled himself up to his full height and pretended to threaten Philip. "Because if you are…"

Philip shrank back, then leaned forward to Jack. "No, no fun about it. They'd like you to start as soon as you can. The pay is good and I don't think you'll be throwing anybody out into the street." Then he had to laugh, "Of course, I think that's the part of this job you like the best, ain't it?"

Jack drew a beer for the impatient customer and slid it down the bar. He untied his apron and tossed it under the bar. "Is tonight soon enough?" At this, he poured himself and Philip each a shot. He would walk out of the Delta and never look back; especially he would never look back at Juliette climbing the stairs.

30.

The Corner Saloon was bustling this evening as plans were being made to celebrate Nevada's new statehood. Ralston, Sharon, Mackay, Fair and the others had been politically out-maneuvered by Abraham Curry, a settler who had envisioned Carson City becoming the capital of the Nevada Territory, now the State of Nevada. He had bought large tracts of land there and even set aside a portion in the center to be the site of the new capitol.

"That Curry, he's a sly one," Ralston told his friends. "Taking Governor Nye through Carson on the way to San Francisco about sealed the deal, I reckon." The others nodded in agreement at Ralston's observation, but the decision still rankled some in the group.

"I say it should be the golden rule," Mackay expounded, and with a rueful chuckle, "Whoever has the gold, or in this case, the silver, should make the rules." Jack brought in a tray of fresh whiskeys for the men while one of the bar girls removed the empty glasses and emptied the crystal ash trays. "No matter, though, we'll show them we know how to throw a party right here that'll make them all look at Carson City as just another wide spot in the road," Mackay boasted.

"We certainly will, gentlemen," Sharon interjected. He had just returned from a trip to Washington where he had met personally with President Lincoln. He stood and adjusted his vest and jacket while the other men quieted. Even Jack lingered an extra moment to hear what the banker would say. "President Lincoln assured me that he will be traveling to Virginia City a month hence, not Carson City." All of the others were astonished, and Jack nearly dropped the tray of glasses. Sharon continued, "I promised him a tour of the mines followed by an evening of entertainment right here in the opera house."

"Hear, hear!" the men said in a chorus, all bursting to speak about what arrangements would need to be made. The finest liquors and delicacies would be brought from San Francisco. The chef from the exclusive Millionaires Washoe Club would be induced to cook for the gala. Should they have a play? Or a concert? Or both? From that moment on the town was abuzz with excitement over the preparations.

In the coming days Juliette discussed the President's upcoming visit with Territorial Enterprise editor Clemens. By now he and Juliette had become fast friends and she had told him her life's story. Clemens, with his newspaperman's natural suspicion of politicians, was no fan of the President, but he could sense Juliette's excitement over an event of such magnitude. "I expect I'll have to go," Clemens said, "but I don't see myself paying any respects." He puffed on his cigar for a moment and added, "In fact, I think I know just the statement to make. I believe I'll take you with me," he said to the prostitute. "After all, you and he have quite a bit in common." Juliette didn't know whether to be offended or amused, but she was frankly astonished when he pulled a one hundred dollar bill out and handed it to her. "Get the most elegant satin and silk dress you can find, something in blue for your eyes, my dear." Clemens' wife had 'taken to her bed' months before and was rarely seen in public. Juliette demurred but Clemens insisted and indeed, two weeks later she did enter the reception for the President on Clemens' arm.

The society ladies were outraged, many of them red in the face with anger, but Juliette maintained her calm decorum. When she greeted many of their husbands by name, it was their turn to be red-faced as well. Jack watched her and felt the pain as deeply as ever, but he grudgingly admired her courage. In the years to come the citizens of Virginia City would look back on the gaiety of that night and wonder if pride did indeed go before a fall. Some six months later President Lincoln would be assassinated and the residents of Virginia City felt it deeply, since many had enjoyed the privilege of shaking his hand.

Now when the bankers and mine owners came to The Corner Saloon there were more worried looks among them and their conversations were far less exuberant. The third shift had been let go at the mill and the silence in the evening became a heavy, foreboding pall that settled over the town. Many wondered when the mill would close completely as fewer and fewer ore carts were brought out of the deep mines.

Later in the year a terrible fire killed hundreds and destroyed nearly half the town, even racing through some of the heavily-timbered mines. Padraig had been among the many dead. The fire started in the wooden shacks on A. Street, the most heavily populated part of town. Thousands were left homeless, although most had little to lose in the way of possessions. And this would not be the worst fire to decimate the town in years to come.

The Delta was spared and became a makeshift hospital with the whores doing what they did best, tend to people. Juliette learned the beloved opera house was lost and yearned to find word of Jack. She knew, of course, that he had always loved her, but she considered him a cherished friend and confidante. Late on the night of the fire Jack staggered into the Delta, soot-covered. Philip and he supported the wardrobe mistress between them, but Jack admitted the bar girls and the shoeshine man had perished in the blaze.

The office of the Territorial Enterprise was destroyed as well, but Juliette's great friend and mentor, Samuel Clemens, was in San Francisco at the time.

Mine owners surveyed the damage in the days to come and pronounced the mines still intact, a pronouncement designed largely to reassure the stock market in San Francisco and keep the investment money pouring in; this was the time when it was needed most, of course as many of the great wooden hoistings would have to be rebuilt and water pumped out of the mine shafts.

But, the town rose slowly from the ashes. Virginia City had been built by people with nothing but hopes and dreams and the willingness to work hard and sacrifice, so if they had to do all that again they would.

No event captured people's belief in the future as much as a wedding held only a month later. Kathleen married Philip in a lovely dress made only for her by her long-time friend, the wardrobe mistress. Jack gave her away and Juliette served as her matron of honor. Flo organized a wedding luncheon that even the Irish attended, although many were still in mourning. Flo announced to Juliette that, indeed, this was her retirement luncheon as well; she was turning the reigns over to Juliette to manage the brothels.

Jack went back to bartending, although this time in the Millionaires' Washoe Club. It was not long after that he was approached by The Big Four, Virginia City's famed bankers. It appeared that all his years of diplomacy practiced behind the bar made him an attractive candidate for a seat in the legislature. He accepted, partly because on the ride to Carson City he could enjoy the sight of herds of wild mustang galloping through the sagebrush.

Book Two

The Rebirth

1.

When Kathleen walked down the aisle of St. Theresa's church to be married to her true love, Philip, she felt half sick and not just due to nerves. She knew she was pregnant with Padraig's child, Padraig having been killed in the Great Fire some eight weeks earlier. She remembered the probable night of this child's conception very well and grimaced with the thought of it, thankful her wedding veil did not betray her emotions.

The mines had closed early in recognition of the founding ceremony that night for E. Clampus Vitus, the Clampers, as they were known, a group that looked out for widows and orphans of miners. Padraig had come home to an empty house, no Kathleen, no dinner on the table, no fire in the hearth. A half-hour later when Kathleen rushed in the house, he was ready for her. "Coming home from the Opera House are ye?" he sneered at her. "Up there making time with the fancy pi-ana player?" She didn't get the first word of a reply out before he hit her with his closed fist. "Don't you think everyone in town knows that you run up there every day to see him?" And he hit her again and again. "And all the fellas in the mine wondering why I don't have no children!" Padraig ripped Kathleen's dress off and threw her on their narrow bed. "Maybe tonight we'll change that!" He raped her again and again, finally leaving her mute, her face turned toward the wall, while he slammed the door and left for the Clampers meeting.

What could she do? There was some truth to what he said. She did go up there nearly every day hoping to spend a few minutes with Philip, listening to him play familiar tunes and work on new compositions. She straightened up his music and fussed over his shirt and jacket for that night's performance, all under the watchful eye of the wardrobe mistress. She felt certain that if they were ever to be alone…

But they never had been, and neither had ever spoken of their true feelings. She wanted to run back up the hill to him, wait outside the stage door and throw herself in his arms. Instead, she set to repairing the table that had been damaged when Padraig first knocked her down. She straightened up the little two-room shack and put a cold rag over her face. She knew she wouldn't be going anywhere for several days until the bruises healed. At least there was food in the house.

That very day Philip had been ready to tell her what he was feeling. As she helped him into his jacket and straightened his cravat, he wanted to take her into his arms, but he kept his head up and looked over her shoulder instead. When she left the Opera House, he went to the stage door and watched her hurry down the hill to the Irish shantytown, hoping she might at least turn and wave at him, give him another glimpse of her face, her flowing red hair catching all the hues of the sunset.

The days that followed were pure hell as the Great Fire decimated much of Virginia City and hit the shantytown hardest of all. Philip had no way of knowing whether Kathleen was dead or alive. Even the Opera House had burned to the ground, so he himself was displaced as well. Heedless of the damage to his bare hands, he tore through the wreckage of the prestigious concert hall, finally discovering the wardrobe mistress clinging to life, buried under a pile of chairs. He dragged her out into the street just when The Corner Bar's head bartender, Jack, emerged from the rubble, carrying the dead body of the shoeshine man.

"I think she's all that survived," Philip said, pointing to Emma, the elderly wardrobe mistress. Jack agreed and the two decided to take her down to C. Street which looked to have been less affected by the fire. As they made their way down the hill they could see the Delta, the Bucket of Blood, and a handful of other saloons still standing. Most of the activity seemed to be at the Delta, and they carried Emma to its swinging doors. A hospital of sorts had been set up with the Delta whores serving as nurses. Two of them took Emma from the men and pointed them to the bar which was doing a brisk business, even in the midst of the crying, bleeding and dying.

"Reckon you'll stay on?" Jack asked Philip, turning his back to the gruesome scene.

"Well, gosh, I hadn't even thought that far." He finished his whiskey and signaled for another and one for Jack as well. "I don't know where I'd go and…" He couldn't finish the sentence out loud with what he was thinking, "I couldn't leave Kathleen."

Juliette interrupted their thoughts. "I'm organizing a rescue group to go down to the Irish town, see who's left down there, what we can do. You boys'll help, won't you?" Of course, Jack couldn't refuse Juliette anything and Philip leapt at the chance to search for his Irish love. They slammed their whiskeys down and followed her out the back of the saloon where other men had rounded up axes, shovels and the like and tied wet bandanas around their face. The flames were mostly out but the ash was thick in the air. A group of ten set off down the hill, not knowing what they would find but expecting the worst.

2.

Kathleen heard the flames before she saw them, a sharp crackling with a whining roar sucking all of the oxygen out of the already soot-black sky. She knew that sitting in the wooden shack would simply be waiting for death and did the only thing she could. She flung herself face-down into the mud puddle in front of her porch that had been the bane of existence ever since they moved in, constantly soiling her shoes and the hem of her dress, stinking and attracting every kind of bug. She dug in as deeply as she could, trying not to swallow the muck and mud as it engulfed her. Kathleen prayed like she never had before, even more than when she was in the black, rolling, stinking hold of the ship crossing from Ireland. It took an eternity for the flames to pass over but finally they did.

She dragged herself upright and looked at what was left. Absolutely nothing. Her house and every one for blocks in each direction were gone. The smoke was too thick to see very far uphill but she wasn't able to pick out the roof of the Opera House and knew it had been lost, too. Kathleen started to walk in the direction of the mines and as she did she encountered more women like herself who had survived based on their wits and determination. One covered herself with a wash basin, another dove into the horse trough. Their faces showed their shock; the worst were those who had lost children in the inferno. "They was playin' out in the street and wouldn't come in," one said, while others just sobbed in guilt, frustration and sadness. "Just wee ones and now they're gone." Another went so far as to tell Kathleen, "Aye, you're the lucky one."

The women singly and in pairs drifted to the intersection of A and Broad Streets and saw that the stone-hewn Catholic church had been saved. Many crossed themselves and recited rosaries. "It's a miracle is what it is," they intoned. By now Kathleen's shock was giving way to another emotion, fear. What would they do now? She forced herself to speak sharply to the women. "It's no miracle. It's a stone building for heaven's sake!" They continued to finger their rosary beads but listened to her. "We have to get to the mines and see if our husbands survived." She began herding them down A Street, trying not to look at the bodies lying in the rubble.

The scene at the entrance to the Chollar mine was no better. Bodies were being carried out of the mine entrance even as the sign at the mouth of the tunnel continued to burn. One of the superintendents stood by, writing in a book as each body was piled by the ore carts. It was impossible to identify many of those retrieved, but he attempted to make some observation about each. "Newer boots." Or, "No undershirt." Kathleen had long ago stopped listening to Padraig when he described which tunnel he had been assigned; it was all the same to her but, now she wished fervently that she had paid more attention. Perhaps he was in one of the very deep tunnels and might be spared. The gathering women sobbed and several fainted. A few identifications were made, one by Kathleen when she saw a charred corpse with a glittering gold cross around its neck. She would recognize the cross anywhere. Padraig claimed his mother had given it to him before they went into the workhouses and he was never without it. She hoped it had given him some comfort as he passed over.

The fire had gone into the mines, incinerating the miners in the upper tunnels while robbing the others of oxygen. In the deeper levels, the tunnels collapsed on the men as the timbers were consumed by the flames. Kathleen wondered idly, which would be the worse death? She gave Padraig's full name to the superintendent and accepted his brusque condolences. He perhaps had known her husband better than she herself had.

Jack, Philip and the other men had fanned out through the shantytown, finding a few poor souls alive but in shock. Many had burns and injuries suffered when houses fell in on them. There were few men, of course, but mostly women and children. The sight of children holding onto their dead mothers' hands nearly made Jack break down. He hoped that when his wife and child were killed that it had been quick and neither had to see the other suffer. Philip was in a private agony. Each time he saw red hair his heart sunk even though he knew many Irish women had red hair (although none as beautiful as Kathleen's, he thought). When they felt they had found all the survivors possible, they led their little band up the hill to the Delta. A few broke off and went to the Catholic church but most were content for the moment just to be led away from the destruction.

3.

Like the others, Kathleen gradually drifted up to C Street, the part of the city least damaged even though the flames could easily have sped down the boardwalk on both sides of the street and taken out nearly every business. The Delta seemed to be where people were congregating, so Kathleen wandered down to the saloon, although she was hesitant to set foot inside until a red-shirted Clamper took her elbow and drew her to one of the tables where other Clampers were taking the names of widows who would need help.

"Why, you're Padraig Kelly's wife, aren't you?" one of the Clampers asked, then crossed himself. "Such a good man now gone." She could do nothing but nod in reply. In all the commotion, Juliette spotted Kathleen, although it wasn't easy given that she was covered in mud and ash. She could tell by the look on the young woman's face what had happened to her lout of a husband. Juliette hated to be uncharitable, especially at a time such as this, but she couldn't help wondering if the fire had done some women a favor.

"I'm so sorry to see you here," Juliette said softly, taking Kathleen's arm and drawing her aside. Kathleen was still too numb to even respond, so Juliette waved one of the other whores over. "Take her up to my room and get her washed up. Put that green dress on her, the one with the stitching on the sleeves." The other young woman guided her up the stairs and did as she was told. After attending to a few of the other new widows, Juliette slipped upstairs and was amazed at the transformation a bath and a clean dress had made.

Kathleen sat at the little dressing table, still dry-eyed, but when she saw Juliette she did start to cry. Her former wagon-mate comforted her as best as possible then made her dry her eyes. "I've got some people downstairs who will be quite happy to see you," she told Kathleen, "so no more tears." She tucked one of Kathleen's curls behind her ear and stood appraising her. "You're a beautiful young woman. With the right clothes and some pretty things, well…"

"Well, what? I could be a whore?" Kathleen still had some fight in her after all. She stammered and started to cry again. "Oh, please, Juliette. I'm so grateful but I'm so scared, too."

"Shush, I know," Juliette answered, patting Kathleen's arm. "Let's go downstairs and be with friends." She led Kathleen to the landing where the whores normally paraded themselves and at that moment Philip chanced to look up. He thought he'd seen an angel. Emma had the exact same thought and they both raced to the foot of the stairs. This time Kathleen didn't hesitate. She threw herself into Philip's arms and just repeated, "Thank God, thank God you're alive!" He held her and only reluctantly surrendered her to Emma for a quick hug.

Juliette surveyed the scene with a knowing eye. She descended slowly to the saloon and thought she might have a little fun with the group. "Yes, Kathleen can stay with me until she decides where she'd like to live," she informed Philip and Emma. "Doesn't she look just lovely, poor dear, with everything she's been through?" and then quickly added, "I mean you've all been through."

"She'll do nothing of the sort!" Emma snorted. "A young lady like her staying in a whorehouse. It's just, just," she fumbled for the right word finally settling on, "unseemly. It's just unseemly." She gripped Kathleen's arm firmly and pronounced. "She will be staying with me, and that's that." For years Emma had stayed in her two rooms at the Mackay mansion in exchange for a little light housekeeping and what not. The rooms were small but the house was grand and she knew Mrs. Mackay would have no objection. Plus which, Emma reasoned, she could do with a little help anyway; she wasn't getting any younger and the shock of the fire would take its toll.

Philip still had done nothing but stare dumbstruck at Kathleen. Stiffly, he finally took her hand, "I'm very sorry for your loss." He went to release her hand, still not looking her in the eye, but she held on and took his other hand as well.

"I hope you will come to see us," Kathleen said lightly. "Emma and I both enjoy your company and I know Mr. Mackay has a piano. Perhaps you can play for us one day." Inwardly she cringed. I sound like a bloomin' idiot arranging a picnic when my husband lies dead less than a day.

Philip agreed that he would indeed come to call on the two ladies, then bid them goodnight and went in search of Jack and another whiskey, or two. Emma meanwhile bustled about Kathleen and Juliette. "We'll be getting this dress back to you straight-away," the seamstress stated. "I'll make the girl a proper dress myself."

Juliette chuckled to herself and flicked away the suggestion. "Oh, no matter, I've got dozens." She paused, "You know a girl needs a few pretty things to make up for all the bad ones."

4.

The constant noise of the stamping mills and the rattling of the ore carts fell silent, replaced by church bells tolling. It was the unaccustomed silence that was harder to deal with than the noise. The bars, and even the whores, continued to do a brisk business, but fist-fights were more common. Jack had gone back to work tending bar at the Delta but spent much of the evening being bouncer, referee, and of course, counselor. Philip sought his advice nearly every night. "What should I do about Kathleen? When should I go see her? Should I go see her?" And on and on it went. Jack urged him to follow his heart but allowed that these were strange times.

"Maybe what would have been proper before ain't so important now," he advised the lovesick young man. "I think you should just be honest." He continued, "Go up there in the middle of the afternoon—not after a whiskey or two—and call on Emma." Kathleen would be there, of course. "Maybe even ask to speak to Mr. Mackay about tuning up his piano or some such other excuse." Philip thought he could possibly do that. He wondered why he was so reticent now about talking to a young woman whose company he had enjoyed many afternoons at the Opera House. Jack read his thoughts. "I know why you're holding back because this time she could really be yours." He poured Philip another drink.

One night Philip felt emboldened by the whiskey and talk of women and asked Jack directly. "What about you? When you going to get yourself a wife?" He'd seen Jack take the occasional whore upstairs but nothing more than that.

Jack glowered. "I had a wife, the best there ever was, and there won't never be another." Even as he swore it, however, Philip saw him look toward the balcony where Juliette waited for another man's attentions.

Philip was back to playing beat-up old pianos in the saloons that had them since the Opera House and its magnificent Steinway had been lost in the fire. At least three nights a week, however, he was able to play at the Millionaires Bar with a much nicer clientele. It was here that the miners and bankers had resorted to meeting as well. They didn't have the luxury of the private room they enjoyed at The Corner Saloon and with the stress of recovering from the town's losses, their conversations could get loud and heated. The mines simply had to be reopened — and fast — the bankers complained. The mine owners answered, as soon as we get the money — and it better be fast — we will.

The fire had spooked the stock market in San Francisco as had rumors that the mines even before the fire had been "chasing the vein," that the silver was, in fact, being depleted. What miners were available were put to work clearing the tunnels and replacing the timbers, arduous work with no pay-off in valuable ore for time being. Water had built up in the deeper tunnels so the owners were faced with the dual problem of how to effectively drain water hundreds of feet deep in the earth. Pumps were barely the answer.

"Did you hear that crazy bastard Sutro got the go-ahead from the State to start his tunnel to drain the mines out somewhere by Dayton?" Ralston asked the others at his table, referring to a little town about six miles down the hillside.

"Well, these times require bold moves, gentlemen," replied Mackay, the seasoned miner and now mine owner. "The only problem is we're going to be much deeper with these new tunnels than his, so we'd be pumping the water up to reach his drainage tunnel, not down." The men enjoyed a brief laugh over what they thought was Fulton's folly.

But Ralston persisted, "He has been able to sell stock quite effectively over in San Francisco. Why, even some of our own miners here are buying in."

Mackay acknowledged that was true. "They say it'll make the mines safer. 'Look what happened at Yellowjacket,' they say." The men at the table grew silent thinking of the 75 miners lost in one shaft fire. "I just don't like him sneakin' up our skirts, havin' another entrance to our mine, is all." The group of powerful men ended the evening committed to buying bigger and better pumps and extending the mines deeper and in greater lateral tunnels. Ralston said he and fellow banker Sharon would journey to San Francisco to calm the fears there.

San Francisco, in fact, seemed more and more appealing to many Virginia City residents, including Philip who felt he could certainly pursue a better paying and more prestigious piano career. He had begun talking to Kathleen about it during the afternoons when they visited under Emma's watchful eye. Kathleen was cautiously supportive of his dreams, not wanting to lose him to the city but not wanting to stand in the way either. Emma had been like a mother to Kathleen, so very little escaped her attention, especially Kathleen's wan appearance each morning and the sound of her being sick to her stomach. She knew what it meant, even if Kathleen didn't.

When Kathleen came into the kitchen the next morning, Emma had a pot of tea and some soda crackers set out on the table. Kathleen looked truly miserable. "Now, now, girl," Emma started gingerly, "we're going to have to talk about what's happening with you."

"Oh, I'm sure it's the rich food here at the mansion and the rememberin' and all," Kathleen answered weakly. "I'll be fine by the time Philip's here this morning to take us on that picnic." With that she retched again and Emma pushed a few crackers on her.

"I'm sure you'll force yourself to be fine with him, dear, but you have to face the fact." She tilted Kathleen's face up to look her in the eye. "You're in the family way. You're going to have a baby." Kathleen looked horrified and pulled away, but Emma persisted. "Now, the question is, who's the father? Padraig or Philip?"

At this, Kathleen could take no more. "Why Philip has never touched me, well except that one hug after the fire. And Padraig…" She sobbed. "Padraig was always on me and nothing like this ever happened. Why now? Oh, Lord, why now?"

"Well, I don't know that the Lord has anything to do with it," Emma answered matter-of-factly, "but you're just going to have to set your mind to it. You're going to be a mother." Then she told the young woman to stop crying and fix her face; after all, Philip was coming to take them out on a picnic that she herself had been greatly looking forward to.

Philip arrived a half-hour later looking as nervous as a long-tailed cat in a room full of rocking chairs, Emma thought. She seated the young man in the parlor and told him Kathleen would be in shortly; she would be just outside in the kitchen. When Kathleen came in there was no evidence of her previous tears and sickness. She looked radiant and Philip told her so. Hesitantly and in a voice so low Kathleen had to ask him to speak up he took her hand. "Before we go on our picnic today, there's something I'd like to ask you." Taking a deep breath, he plunged ahead, "Kathleen Kelly, will you marry me?"

Emma rushed into the parlor, "She will! She will!" the seamstress gushed while Kathleen sat mute. "Now just tell this nice young man you will," she prodded Kathleen who looked ready to faint.

"I can't," Kathleen said in a hush. "I can't because I'm carrying another man's baby."

Philip was appropriately surprised but recovered in an instant. "Oh, Kathleen, you'll be a wonderful mother and that child needs a father." Emma thought it might be her turn to faint, but Philip swept the tearful Kathleen into his arms and said, "We'll be a family and I'll do everything to take care of the both of you." Emma hoped he might have been referring to her when he said 'the both of you' but realized he meant the baby, of course.

So, Kathleen found herself a few weeks later approaching the altar and wondering what kind of a person a child conceived in such violence would become.

She wasn't alone in her sense of foreboding that day. There were problems with the very deep tunnels, and perhaps there were things in them that were also conceived in violence and should not have been disturbed.

5.

Jack began to see that the deeper the tunnel the men worked in during the day, the harder they drank at night. He supposed they were constantly terrified of being buried alive, caught in a fire, drowned, or even killed by one of their former miners in an apparent 'accident'. It happened, as petty disputes took on greater significance in the deepest shafts where temperatures could be 100 degrees or more and every swing of a pick threatened to bring down the whole mountain.

Tensions were running high everywhere, it seemed. Even Philip, normally a mild-mannered former farm boy seemed nervous as his wedding day approached. "Oh, I know it will be wonderful having Kathleen as my wife," he confided to Jack, "but I worry all the time that I won't be able to provide for her the way she'd like."

"The way she'd like or the way you'd like?" Jack asked pointedly. "She's had it rough ever since she and her father left Ireland, so even living with the likes of you will be an improvement." He laughed and tried to lighten the mood but Philip was having none of it.

"And then with the baby…" Philip blushed the second he realized he'd let the cat out of the bag. "I mean if we were ever to have a baby, you know." Jack said nothing and Philip realized he had to unburden himself to someone. "She's pregnant and feelin' pretty badly about it." Jack raised an eyebrow so that Philip quickly had to correct things. "It's Padraig's baby. We've never so much as kissed."

"Well, you're a good man then for taking that on," Jack assured him. "She's got some pluck in her and she'll come around to being a mother, you watch."

"Who's going to be a mother?" Juliette had been standing behind Philip and neither man had noticed her. "Who? Come on, you can tell me."

Jack huffed. "Might as well just take an ad out in the Enterprise as tell you anything that's a secret."

"Oooh, it's a secret," she cooed. "Better yet, now you have to tell me!"

"Kathleen is going to kill me!" Philip sighed. "You can't say a word to anyone, especially not to her," he entreated Juliette who was, in fact, planning a wedding shower for Kathleen the very next day.

"Oh, nonsense," Juliette laughed. "Mum's the word," making the sign of locking her lips with a key and then throwing it away. She wondered about the old rumors of Philip and Kathleen having an affair but decided not to press it with the future groom who was clearly distressed. "We ladies are going to have a lovely afternoon tomorrow, and then Saturday you'll be united with your lovely bride." The Mackays had graciously offered their parlor for the shower, although Mrs. Mackay thought it would be scandalous and might very well appear in the next Tattler column — a whore playing hostess in the mansion on the hill!

She flounced off with a little laugh while both men shuddered. Juliette could play the fool, but Jack knew she was anything but. He'd heard the rumors that Flo was planning to turn the brothel over to Juliette; he knew it would be a good business decision but it would certainly spell the end of his days at the Delta. The owner of the Millionaires' Washoe Club had been pressuring him to make a change anyway.

Tensions ran high in Emma's rooms at the Mackay mansion, too. Emma had sewn a stunning wedding dress for Kathleen but the bride-to-be burst out in tears every time she had to try it on for another fitting. "Oh, I just know I'm going to be walkin' down the aisle with my stomach out to here and everyone talkin' about me," she cried.

"Oh, you foolish girl," Emma chided her. "You're not showing at all and won't be for another month!" Kathleen's sobs were replaced by little hiccups and the older woman felt ashamed for chiding her. With her arm around Kathleen's shoulders, she tried to comfort her. "You've got a good man now and a new start in life, and when that baby comes it'll be the happiest day of your life, you'll see." Kathleen had come to love Emma like a mother so she allowed herself to be comforted and tried the shimmering satin dress on one more time. Emma had copied the design from a French catalogue she found in Mrs. Mackay's drawing room and certainly there would never be one like it in Virginia City!

6.

Jack began to see that the deeper the tunnel the men worked in during the day, the harder they drank at night. He supposed they were constantly terrified of being buried alive, caught in a fire, drowned, or even killed by one of their former miners in an apparent 'accident'. It happened, as petty disputes took on greater significance in the deepest shafts where temperatures could be 100 degrees or more and every swing of a pick threatened to bring down the whole mountain.

The men half-jokingly referred to their work as taking them one step closer to hell. The hissing steam seemed to almost be talking to them at times, and the rumbling in the tunnels seemed also to take on a life of its own. They couldn't wait to be hoisted to the surface after their shift and some said if they were to turn back and look at the shaft they'd see the devil himself bidding them good night.

Actually, they wouldn't be far from the truth. Only inches of rock separated them from an equally malevolent being, one that was becoming increasingly annoyed. Vicente found the sound of the picks chipping away, the men shouting at one another, the clanging of lunch pails banging against the tunnel walls—all of it—just subtly escalating his violent urges. The rocky tomb that had been his resting place for dozens...hundreds perhaps? of years was about to be breached. He could feel it. But as he lay there in the darkness Vicente wondered, was that good or bad? Was it time for him to go out into the world again? He had been cast out of The Family long ago because of certain, shall we say, indiscriminate behaviors. He had roamed on his own, traveling West, until the sameness of the barren desert finally bored him to death (although clearly he was dead already, he laughed to himself; good, he still had his sense of humor!). He finally just decided to hole up in a cave and take the long sleep. Now these wretches had awakened him and he was determined to find out why.

He pushed aside the tons of rock concealing his tomb and stepped out into the shaft, following the fresh air to its opening to the night sky. He was astonished to see thousands of twinkling lights on the hill above. It was a city, by God. It certainly wasn't Athens, or even its shabby cousin, Rome, but it was a city. He stood there breathing in the fresh air, a hint of sage and more than a hint of dust, but that, of course, could be coming from himself. Vicente brushed off his dark suit and adjusted his cuffs. The sapphire cufflinks caught the moonlight so nicely, he noticed. The longer he stood at the tunnel entrance, the more strongly he felt it—a powerful life force much greater than anything the miners had exuded for certain. Vicente found himself drawn inexorably up the hill to the ramshackle little city.

Juliette, meanwhile, was sitting at her dressing table looking out her window to the vast expanse of desert below. Perhaps it was the full moon, but certainly it felt like something was drawing her to the view. She mused that perhaps she was becoming like Jack, enchanted with the desert after all. He used to take her out to watch the mustang herds and said that was when he felt the most calm and contented. She looked back on those trips now and realized how petty she had been, complaining about every speck of dirt and every sagebrush that snagged her skirt. Jack was a good man and she had sorely abused his affection, she knew. Enough of these maudlin thoughts! It was time to go back downstairs and see how her girls were doing. Since Flo had turned over the business to her, she really did feel proprietary about the whores.

Vicente strolled the boardwalk in front of the saloons and was relieved to find out he needn't worry about the style of his suit; it appeared he might be the only person in town to own one! He stepped neatly aside as a rowdy drunk was pushed unceremoniously out of an establishment called The Bucket of Blood. My, how interesting is that? But, it turns out it was just another saloon, and a pretty rundown one at that. Most of the activity seemed to be at "Virginia City's Famous Delta Saloon and Brothel." So, this was Virginia City. He liked the sound of the name. As he passed by tethered horses he noted he still had the ability to spook them. Well, you haven't lost that either, old boy. Horses, he had to admit, were rather smarter than they looked; cows were another story entirely.

As he ruminated in front of the Delta, the life force drawing him flared up again with a vengeance, and as soon as he pushed through the doors, he immediately knew why. He saw the most lovely creature, a fine-boned young woman with raven-black hair and turquoise eyes, glittering to match his cufflinks. She took his breath away. He felt rooted to the spot, unable to approach her but unable to turn away. He watched as the woman who was called Juliette took a wad of bills from one of the ruffians, then led him by the hand upstairs. Ah! She was a courtesan. How wonderful! He resolved to wait until she came back down the stairs and with his uncanny speed he was able to lift a few coins off a table of card-playing men so he could purchase a drink. He didn't think he could actually blend in, but he would try, in his dark and, he just noticed, dusty suit. His hair was worn long and still quite lustrously black. It at least appeared to be in fashion, although most of the men wore hats (indoors, what boors!).

Well, obviously this was no five-minute rendezvous, Vicente mourned. He decided to be a bit more daring and sat down to play poker with the men. In no time, he had amassed a pile of chips, coins and bills and a few threatening stares. No matter. If you can cheat death, you can cheat at cards, he reasoned.

Finally the nymph reappeared and Vicente wasted no time in approaching her. "Ah, miss, I wonder if I might…" Might what? He was no longer capable of acting sexually although he still considered himself a sensualist.

"It's ten dollars for a straight poke," Juliette said bluntly, taking in his old-fashioned suit and odd coloration. "More if you want something special."

"Oh, yes, most assuredly I *do* want something special," Vicente replied with a low rumble to his voice. How odd it was to be talking aloud after all these years.

"Well, come on then, let's get to it," Juliette said, snatching a handful of bills from him and directing him to the stairs. "First thing, though, is you must let me wash you up."

Ah, Vicente thought, it would be lovely to have my hair shampooed. But, horrors, that was not at all what Juliette had in mind. When she reached for his fly he thought he might faint. "No, no, that's not necessary," he stammered. "All I would really like to do is, is, um, brush your hair, if I might."

In her years as a whore Juliette had been asked to do some pretty peculiar things, and if the price was right, she often went along, but this was a new one. Brush my hair? The stranger directed her to her dressing table and picked up the silver brush lying there. Gently, gently he pulled the brush through her curls, now and then lifting them off her neck and letting them fall where they might. His hands were as cold as ice, actually a nice feeling given the stifling heat of the summer evening. Vicente was long past the need to feed, as it were, so Juliette was in no immediate danger from him. She tried to make small talk with him, asked him where he was from, what brought him to Virginia City, and all that. He decided to keep his answers vague and simply told her he was from Spain and was out West to "take the airs." His responses seemed to satisfy her but after perhaps a quarter of an hour, she told him it was time for her to go back downstairs. "If you leave those whores on their own for too long, they'll be talkin' the bartender out of free drinks and giving away 'samples' to the customers," she informed him.

"Ah, just so," he agreed. "Perhaps another evening then?"

"If you've got the money, honey, I've got the time," Juliette replied in her lilting English accent, all the while leading him back down to the saloon.

He cursed himself when he stepped back out onto the boardwalk. Brush her hair! You imbecile. You couldn't come up with anything better than that! But then he reminded himself. You can't take life too seriously because, after all, you're dead. Hah! That joke never gets old, Vicente chuckled to himself and set off down the hill, back to his tomb.

7.

The wedding went off without a hitch, and as Jack had predicted, Flo used the luncheon afterwards to announce her and Mr. Wynn's decision to turn the Delta brothel over to Juliette who acted surprised but confided in Jack later that she already had a list of "improvements" she planned to make, some of them even involving the bar. Jack made up his mind right then to seek out the owner of the Millionaires' Club and ask for a job. He had been Philip's best man and Juliette was her maid of honor, but that was as close as he was ever likely to get to Juliette and thought it would be better to have her out of his sight.

The newlyweds announced their intention to move to San Francisco and within a week they were gone. They had asked Emma to go with them to be a nanny and companion, but the old seamstress decided a baby was too much responsibility, and besides, the Opera House was being rebuilt and they would need new costumes soon. She bid Philip and Kathleen a teary farewell. Even John Mackay came out to wish the couple well and he pressed a list of names in Philip's hand for him to contact in San Francisco. Juliette did not come by the mansion but sent word that she would likely see them in San Francisco as she had 'grand shopping trip' in mind to redecorate the Delta brothel. As she had always maintained, a few pretty things can offset a lot of bad, and heaven knows the girls deserved it for what they went through.

As she boarded the Virginia and Truckee Railroad, or the V & T as the locals dubbed it, Kathleen certainly had mixed emotions. She was leaving behind the only friends she had ever known as an adult, but she was also leaving the sight of her dead husband and the horrors of surviving the fire herself.

Jack had missed the gathering at the mansion as he was at the Millionaires' Club ensuring his employment there, but he did come by the train station, giving Philip a hearty slap on the back and Kathleen a heartfelt hug; the girl had been through a lot and he hoped San Francisco would give her the life she deserved. He was surprised when the train pulled slowly out of the station that he felt the sudden urge to jump on board and begin a new chapter of his life as well. The feeling passed when Jack thought of how much he enjoyed the solitude of the desert as well as hunting and fishing trips in the Sierras, a day's ride west. He didn't suppose the city life would be nearly as appealing.

Life was returning to some semblance of normal in Virginia City as the mine tunnels damaged by the fire were shored up and new ones begun. About half of the men returned to work in the mines while others were sent down to the Carson Valley and to the area around Reno to work logging the Sierras and filling the log flumes with as much timber as possible; houses need to be rebuilt and the tunnels required a tremendous amount of wood as well.

Dozens of trains pulled into the V & T depot each day bringing newer and more powerful equipment for the mills and the mines. The biggest Cornish steam engines made were unloaded and quickly assembled to begin pumping water out of the mines, Sutro's tunnel notwithstanding. A daily topic of conversation revolved around how Virginia City could be looking out on a vast desert yet pumping out thousands of gallon of water each day. Visitors would be hard-pressed to find a tree of any magnitude in the city although the hills were dotted with the scrubby, gnarled pinion pine and mesquite that were useless for any building but did fuel a hot-burning fire.

Of course, the trains also brought people to town, not so many miners now but businessmen and more than a few opportunists who saw money to be made in the rebirth of the frontier town. One of these was Wild Bill Ward, a card shark, occasional horse thief, and all around con man. Wild Bill, or WB as he referred to himself, would turn Virginia City on its head.

8.

As Vicente sauntered along he heard a strange sound. It was…whistling. By gosh, he was whistling! He couldn't remember the last time he had done that. "I must be in high spirits after all," he grinned, "even after that rather embarrassing showing with the courtesan." He resolved to think of another way to spend time with her besides brushing her hair, even though that was rather nice. Should it be tomorrow night? Would he appear too eager? All these thoughts and more were going through his mind as he slipped into the mine and made his way back to his chamber, having carefully concealed the entrance when he left earlier in the evening. His super-human strength made it child's play to roll the boulders back in place, and just for good measure, he added a few more in hopes of drowning out the noise of the mining operations. As he drifted off to sleep he had the thought that he could just pop out when the miners were leaving, grab one and scare the hell out of the rest of them. He'd get some quiet then all right. Vicente dismissed the idea, however, as he wanted to be able to go to town, not tomorrow night, but soon.

Of course, there was the matter of his wardrobe to attend to. Apparently a well-made black suit can go out of style after all. Oh, but how he loved the feel of the silk and velvet against his skin. He shuddered at the thought of "fitting in" and having to endure those rough denim trousers, and worse yet, flannel shirts over scratchy full-length underwear. He would have to slip into the closets of the town's well-to-do — there must be a few such men — and inspect the labels in their clothing. He resolved to do it tomorrow evening.

When the next night set in, Vicente did just that. He had noticed a few more substantial brick and stone houses set up on the hill overlooking the commercial district, and cloaking himself in invisibility, he slipped into one and then another, making note of the names of tailors, all of whom seemed to be in some place called San Francisco. Luckily, one of the homes he visited on his nocturnal prowl belonged to a railroad man, a Mr. Huntington, who had maps spread across his desk indicating the exact location of this San Francisco. Vicente could even take the train! What fun! Of course, traveling in the daytime would be problematic. He would have to watch the trains and see if there were any cars without windows. That would be just the ticket indeed.

In the meantime, he could find a likely victim, a 44-Long, and "appropriate" his clothing, but no, that might be too messy and he had promised to behave in the hopes of being reaccepted by The Family. He accepted his banishment with his head held high, but the indignity of it still stung, and truth be told, he missed the old crowd. The mortals he had encountered seemed rather coarse in comparison. Even the courtesan seemed a bit corrupted, but he supposed the job could do that to a woman.

His inspection of the mansions complete, Vicente once again went back to his tomb satisfied that he had a plan in place. Tomorrow night he would go to the railroad office and see about renting a shipping car for the two-day journey to San Francisco. He would rent a room for a few nights in Virginia City and have a comfy container delivered there; it could be picked up with him in it and subsequently and taken to the train. He would be disappointed to miss the scenery but bursting into flames in the sunlight would have been equally disappointing. Ah, so many little details to consider.

9.

Philip enjoyed the train ride to San Francisco, but for Kathleen, still suffering from morning sickness, it was too reminiscent of her voyage across the ocean. The rolling of the train and the endless clicking and clacking was more annoying than soothing, and she thought if she saw one more pine tree she might scream. To her, the sameness of the desert was no worse than the sameness of the Sierra Nevada forests, although the mountains provided some relief. Philip tried to reassure her that once the train reached San Francisco everything would be much better. He already had an offer to play piano in one of the city's tonier supper houses, and they had been told about which sections of town might be best to look for a house. He hoped to avoid the Irish section although he knew Kathleen would have an easier time making friends there which she would sorely need once the baby arrived.

The baby had already become a point of contention between them. Kathleen made no secret about the fact that she hoped it "wouldn't stick," and Philip had to make her promise to do nothing to cause that result. Everyone assured the young couple that motherhood was the most natural thing in the world and that Kathleen would "take to it" just like other women, but even Philip was having his doubts. He wondered if the child had been his own if she would have felt differently, and he worried that if she didn't take to this child there might not be the opportunity to have one of his own.

When they got their first glimpse of San Francisco Philip was immediately captivated; he hadn't realized how much he missed the ocean, having been a boy in Boston. He resolved to find a house with a view of the Bay and after only two nights in a boarding house, he did find a place on what was called Russian Hill, so named for a Russian graveyard found atop the hill, a fact he didn't share with superstitious Kathleen. She complained about the walk up the steep hill and when the fog rolled in she felt her mood plummet even further. She had no one to talk to in the neighborhood, the residents being mostly older and established. She pestered Philip to move to where the Irish congregated, but he refused, instead leaving earlier and earlier every day for work. Kathleen knew she was being a bad wife and even though she loved Philip madly, she felt powerless to change her behavior or her mood.

Just when Kathleen felt she could stand it no longer she got an unexpected visitor. Juliette had indeed come to San Francisco on a "grand buying spree" and chanced to have dinner in the supper club where Philip was playing. He entreated her, "Oh, you must come visit Kathleen, please. She's been so out of sorts ever since we got here." Juliette reflected on how she had been alternately shunned and avoided to now be sought-after company, but she agreed to visit the following afternoon, only if Philip agreed to let it be a surprise.

When Kathleen cautiously opened the door the next afternoon, she was speechless to see the elegantly coiffed Juliette and burst immediately into tears. "Oh, will you look at me? I'm a mess," she said through her tears, trying to apologize for the drab smock she was wearing, and indeed had worn almost every day for the last three months. Juliette hugged her and tried to make sense of what she saw. Kathleen had always been proud of her appearance, especially her hair which now hung in a lank ponytail halfway down her back. The smock was shabby and the house, even though it was in a nice neighborhood, was in disarray.

Thinking she would brighten the mood, she inquired gently, "And when is the baby due?" That only elicited a fresh round of sobbing as Kathleen tried to explain that she had had no other women to talk to and only a vague idea of what to expect. She made it clear to Juliette, however, that she wanted to be among her own people and if she had to walk to the Irish part of town when the baby was ready to be born, by God she would! Being English, of course, Juliette retained her lack of respect, if not outright contempt, for the Irish, but she felt for Kathleen as a woman and pondered about how best to help her, short of taking her back to Virginia City.

One thing Juliette did know how to do was to recruit women, of course, being always on the look-out for a fresh whore. So, she reasoned, the best thing would be to get an Irish girl to come live with Kathleen and Philip to help with the household and ultimately the baby. She helped Kathleen straighten up a little bit and vowed to return the next afternoon. Kathleen clung to her as she climbed into her carriage, but she knew Juliette as a woman of her word and felt a glimmer of hope, the first in months.

Juliette felt that her own lot in life had not been the best but once again reminded herself, it could always be worse. Back at her hotel she inquired among the housekeeping staff if they knew of a likely young Irish girl who would be a good candidate. In less than an hour there was a timid knock her door and a young woman who could have been Kathleen's older sister presented herself. "I'm Fiona Graham from Cork and I understand you're looking for live-in help?" Kathleen explained the situation and ascertained that Fiona had experience not only taking care of babies but actually as a midwife as well. Things were looking up. They agreed on a small salary and Juliette told the woman to be ready at noon the following day.

Of course, neither Juliette nor Kathleen considered what Philip's reaction might be to another woman living under his roof.

10.

Vicente realized he had rushed his departure from Virginia City; he was simply so rattled by meeting the lovely courtesan and then making such an utter fool of himself with her. Instead of traveling in style, he found himself in a rough wooden shipping container shoved onto a rail car loaded with pigs! Oh, if his friends could see him now, he thought ruefully. He had arranged for his container to be loaded into a warehouse once in San Francisco. There he would simply wait for night to fall and then extricate himself from the odious container and find more suitable lodging in the City. He didn't know quite how he was going to rid himself of the eau d' swine smell, but perhaps the salt air would be enough to camouflage it. In the meantime he would simply endure the ordure, he thought. "Oh, I really do have a way with words!"

Two nights later he slipped out of the warehouse and was quite pleased to see a sizeable city arrayed on hills overlooking the water. All the hills rather reminded him of Rome, in fact. He discerned the financial district was clearly where the grandest buildings were clustered in the center of the city and proceeded to slip into one of the banks under the cover of darkness. Getting in the vault presented little difficulty, and he was thus able to finance his stay in the city, and more. How he loved to shop. A hotel aptly named the Palace was within walking distance of the banks and brokerage houses, he saw, and ventured into the lobby. The desk clerk turned his nose up at Vicente, which could have been the result of his odor, his out-of-date suit, or just the lateness of the hour, but after a flash of the cash a suitable suite of rooms was found. He explained that his luggage would be along later and in the meantime, he was not to be disturbed.

Vicente luxuriated in a warm bath scented with lavender, washing his hair three times. The warmth truly didn't penetrate his hardened cold skin, but it still felt like a decadent thing to do, soaking for hours in candlelight. When he was clean, he crawled into the large bed and drew the velvet bed curtains around it. Before getting into the tub he had sent his suit down to be cleaned and returned the following evening, not before. He also left instructions with the now-unctuous (read that, well-tipped, Vicente thought in disgust) desk clerk to have a tailor summoned from Brooks Brothers the next evening at eight. He could sense that San Francisco was a sophisticated city to be savored tastefully, like fine wine. Just thinking of wine caused him another little tinge because, of course, he could no longer drink wine; he wished he had known *that* little detail before agreeing to accept the 'kiss of the immortals'!

The tailor assured him he was a perfect 44-long and he complimented Vicente's selection of the finest wools and silks. His new wardrobe was ready in days so Vicente was able to begin exploring the grand neighborhoods as well as the seedy haunts along the waterfront. He realized he was delaying his return to the bustling mining town, but at the same time he simply had to see Juliette again and make her realize he was no buffoon. This time, however, there would be no train trip across the Sierras. He ordered a custom-made coach with thick velvet draperies to be drawn by a perfectly matched set of four black stallions, explaining to the coach-builder that he wanted to shield his lovely bride from the prying eyes of the unwashed masses. Again, money swept away any impediments. Soon, he would be back at the Delta, a new man at least in the eyes of who he had begun to think of as *his* courtesan.

11.

The high-spirited black stallions and the exquisite cloaked carriage caused a commotion everywhere Vicente went, even in San Francisco where people feigned a certain sophistication and tried not to stare openly. He was certain that his arrival in Virginia City would warrant a few paragraphs in the Territorial Enterprise's Tattler column at the very least. A parade in his honor was too much to hope for, of course, maybe just an evening soiree with the City's finest? Vicente loved his fantasies and loved being the center of them. He pictured the lovely Juliette on his arm, sweeping down the staircase…no, sweeping down the staircase of a brothel simply ruined the picture. He would have to get a mansion. Certainly there must be some mine owner about to give it all up? First things first. He must return to Virginia City and spend another evening with his enchantress.

The trip over the Sierras was harrowing, not so much for Vicente as for his coachman. The stallions were powerful and not easily controlled, but their skittishness was magnified by their knowledge of the coach's special passenger. At several points the coachman feared the stallions would leap to their death, pulling him and the coach with them off a cliff. They thundered right past mountain lakes which normally would have enticed them to stop and drink their fill of the clear, cold water. It was as if they couldn't get to Virginia City fast enough and disgorge the man behind the velvet curtains.

In record time the coach drew up in front of the Delta, just after sundown. Predictably, half of the customers emptied out into the street to see the spectacle. Even the whores came down off the balcony, all vying to charm the occupant into spending an hour or so—and $10—in their company. Juliette, hearing the ruckus, emerged from her room quite aggravated to see none of the whores on display and the saloon half-empty. Her temper had brought color to her cheeks and that evening she happened to be in a dazzling burgundy velvet dress, so when Vicente first saw her he nearly swooned with desire and delight.

Her reaction on seeing him was not what he expected. The saucy wench laughed out loud! He was quite incapable of blushing, of course, but he knew the reason for her laughter—the hair-brushing incident. Nevertheless, he approached her boldly with a $100 bill in hand. "A moment of your time, perhaps?" She snatched the bill out of his hand like a parrot reaching for a cracker, then linked her arm through his as they climbed the stairs to her boudoir.

"So, what will be your pleasure this evening?" she purred.

"No, not *my* pleasure," Vicente purred back, "it will be your pleasure." With that, he bade her sit down on a pretty little chair and he put the "washing up" basin at her feet, selecting some lilac water from her dressing table with which to perfume it. On his knees in front of her, he unlaced her dainty little slippers. He then gently folded her dress and slip up over her knees, instructing her to hold it thus. She actually blushed from the intimacy of the act as he slid his cool hands up her thighs to undo the garters holding up her stockings, then slowly began to draw them down her legs.

Good lord! Had this woman never heard of a depilatory? The black hair on her legs reminded him of the stallions waiting restlessly out front. If there were hooves at the end of her legs he would not have been surprised! He felt like summoning a barber, telling him to bring an extra blade and strop. He hoped his revulsion wasn't revealed on his face and was glad he could bend his head to his task, away from her view. But if that wasn't enough, when he finally removed the stockings he was further appalled. She could run barefoot up a sheer rock cliff by digging in those toenails! They were as thick as a coin, gnarled and twisted.

Juliette meanwhile evinced no embarrassment or reluctance to have him see her thus. "I usually leave all this on with my customers," she said quite simply as he placed one foot and then the other in the scented water. He had thought to gently bathe what he expected to be exquisite little feet, but this was a different chore altogether. He searched her table for a file and began the odious task of trimming her nails; a blacksmith might have been better suited to the job.

Finally satisfied that he had done as much as possible to remediate the situation, he brought one foot to his mouth and slowly, slowly began to run his tongue up the bottom of her sole. She squealed in delight, something heard all the way down in the saloon, he suspected. His leathery tongue stroked and stroked first one foot, then the other, until all the calluses had been sloughed away. For the first time in eons he was happy not to be a sexual being anymore. Who could have performed under these circumstances? He felt he should be given a public service award for having shielded the men of Virginia City from ever viewing such a spectacle as her rough feet and hairy legs.

Oh, how could he be so drawn, so bewitched by such a contradiction of a woman?

12.

Before Juliette left San Francisco she came by one last time to visit with Kathleen. She had heard from Philip that the baby, a boy, had been born and was, unfortunately, the spitting image of his father, Padraig. Philip didn't think he would have any trouble raising another man's son because he loved Kathleen so dearly, but he found that the very sight of the child annoyed him. When he was home, which was less and less often, he insisted that Fiona take the boy, named Patrick, into another room. The birth had been difficult for Kathleen and she spurned any attempt at affection from Philip; nor would she nurse the baby or even hold it for more than a few minutes.

Fortunately, Fiona bonded with Patrick instantly and marveled at every little movement or gesture the infant made. She thought Philip was quite handsome as well and spent hours sitting in the bay window coddling the baby and imaging the life she and Philip might have; if only he loved the child, but he clearly did not so the whole situation was impossible. When Juliette came to visit, Fiona found herself wishing she would leave and take Kathleen with her back to the Irish shantytown in Virginia City.

Interestingly enough, Kathleen was wishing the same thing. To distract Kathleen a bit from her obvious misery, Juliette had brought in the samples of all the beautiful silks and damasks she had bought to be used for draperies, gowns and upholstery in the brothel. The sight of the rich fabrics had the opposite effect on Kathleen as they reminded her of her friend, Emma, the seamstress, and of the happy afternoons she had spent sewing with her and hearing Philip play the piano in the old opera house.

"Oh, Juliette, they're marvelous!" Kathleen said, trying to stifle a fresh round of tears. "I wish I was going to be sewing them up for you."

Juliette could see in an instant where the conversation was headed. "Oh, now, you've got plenty of sewing ahead of you, making baby clothes for that little bundle," she suggested.

"Oh, pish, Fiona can do that," Kathleen replied shortly. "What difference does it make what some baby wears anyway?"

She shouldn't have been shocked, but she was. "That's not *some* baby, it's *your* baby," she admonished the new mother. "And it's much more important that your child is loved and tended to than what the inside of a whorehouse looks like!"

Kathleen knew Juliette was right but just couldn't bring herself to accept it, and as if on cue, Patrick let out a wail. Fiona comforted the boy and watched Kathleen ignore him once again. Why couldn't this silly girl see what a blessing she had?

When Fiona had left the two women alone, Kathleen turned to Juliette. "You're so smart and so sweet, don't you think you'll ever stop…"

"Whoring?" Juliette replied. "Oh probably. Least-wise I don't do anymore $10 pokes now that I'm running the place." She sighed. "You know, after all I've seen and done and heard about men, I could never trust one." She thought of Jack but put him out of her mind as she had many times before. She leaned in and said conspiratorially, "Now listen, I have a secret to tell you but you mustn't tell anyone, especially Philip."

"Oooh, how delicious. I don't know when I've heard a secret last!" Kathleen exclaimed and clapped her hands together, looking more like the young girl she really was.

"I am going to open my own brothel," Juliette confided. "I have a new customer who seems quite wealthy and quite smitten, if you know what I mean." Kathleen nodded. "I have a plan to get a mansion and outfit it with billiards tables, a card room, a smoking lounge, you know, all first-class."

"Oh, you'll make it grand, I just know," Kathleen said a little wistfully but still excited for her friend whose eyes positively lit up when she began telling her plans. "Tell me about your new customer. Would he be your partner…or your partner?"

"Actually, he's quite peculiar and I've only entertained him once." Then she laughed. "All he wanted to do was brush my hair! Can you imagine?" Both of the women were in hysterics as Juliette described the stranger, who despite his oddness, seemed quite cultured.

"Now, not a word of any of this to Philip," Juliette made Kathleen promise. "You know he sees people from Virginia City in the supper house, and I wouldn't want him to let the cat out of the bag before I'm ready." The two old friends hugged at the door and Juliette went down the stairs to her carriage, turning once again to wave goodbye. She hoped Kathleen would come around to being a mother, but part of her doubted it would ever happen. She also wondered if her finding Fiona had been a blessing or a threat to Kathleen.

13.

The daily doings in Virginia City had been enlivened quite a bit with the arrival of Wild Bill Ward. As soon as he stepped off the train he instinctually headed toward the busiest part of town, the boardwalk fronting the saloons, the Delta in particular. He set up a little table and from his valise drew a bright cloth to cover it and a dozen bars of plain old soap which he set carefully on the table. A small crowd began to form to watch such a curious thing. Wild Bill, or WB, then took out his billfold and extracted a half-dozen bills, which he fanned for the crowd to see. There was at least one hundred dollar bill and several twenties along with a scattering of smaller denominations. These he carefully wrapped individually around perhaps half the bars of soap.

Then, reaching into the valise again he drew out a dozen pieces of wrapping paper and a bolt of twine. He took his pocketknife out and set it on the table. Using the tablecloth to cover the bars of soap he wrapped each bar of soap, tying them with twine and setting each out on the table, all the while never saying a word to the curious onlookers. Finally, when all was set, he called to them. "Ladies and gents, who among you would like to have an extra bit of money in their purse or pocket today?" Everyone nodded but no one said anything until one man spoke up.

"What's the trick?"

"Why no trick at all!" WB responded loudly, then lowering his voice, "just a little luck is all. You simply give me one dollar and point to the bar of soap you choose." He grinned broadly. "Will it have a hundred dollar bill or just a twenty?" He waited for a response and then added, "Would twenty dollars be a good return on your investment of only one dollar?" He winked, "And, you can keep the soap, too."

Finally one man stepped forward and put a silver dollar on the table, pointing to a bar in the middle of the table. "I'll take that one there." WB took out his pocketknife once more and with a flourish said, "Allow me," snipping the twine, then handing the partially unwrapped bar to the man who could continue to unwrap it himself. When the wrapping paper was removed, the man had himself a five-dollar bill and a huge smile.

The crowd was clearly more excited and another man stepped up to WB's little table, also putting down a silver dollar and selecting a bar at the edge of the table. He already had his own knife out and slit into the package. "Lordy, it's a hundred dollars!" and he waved the bill for all to see. A rush of men and even a couple women surged forward to buy their own bars. A few got a dollar bill but most got nothing but the momentary excitement.

Later that afternoon WB met with the man who had "won" the hundred dollar bill, getting it back from him. "I'm telling you, Jake, this is a good little trick," WB said to his partner in the swindle while they enjoyed a beer in a bar some distance from the Delta.

"Oh, it's all right but it's small potatoes," Jake the Snake, as he was known, complained. "These short cons work a few times but then it's back on the road. We gotta come up with something bigger, get us a real stake." WB acknowledged that with the towns in the West being so far from each other, it wasn't as simple as just moving a few miles to the next town to set up the con.

"Well, when Louie gets here tomorrow we'll talk about it again," WB reassured his long-time fellow con man. "I've gotta go buy me some more soap."

Meanwhile in the Millionaires' Club Jack was hearing an earful about that afternoon's entertainment. He'd seen the same con pulled when he and Matthews were riding the riverboats and he suspected his old acquaintance, Wild Bill, was in town and would soon be joined by the rest of his crew. No one's wallet would be safe. The sheriff and a couple of the bankers came in for their usual late afternoon whiskey and parlay, so Jack pulled the sheriff aside. "Say, there's a couple of bad characters come to town you best keep an eye out for," Jack explained. The sheriff had already heard about the little show in front of the Delta that afternoon but hadn't realized it for a con. He hurried back to the table to tell the bankers about it (of course telling them that he knew it'd been a trick all along).

When Jack brought a fresh round of whiskeys to the table, one of the bankers, Ralston, looked up at the bartender they'd all known for a couple of years now. He got the other men's attention and then said, "You know, Jack here's a stand-up fella who's always helping someone out. I think he might be just who we're looking for." Jack couldn't imagine what they were talking about, but they all seemed to murmur in agreement. "We're looking for a man such as yourself, honest as the day is long, hard-working and diplomatic — but a straight-talker — that we can put up for a seat in the new legislature representing the whole county here."

Jack flushed with embarrassment. "I ain't into no speechifying or anything of the sort," he stuttered. "I don't know how you'd settle on the likes of me." Ralston sensed his uneasiness and rather than torment him any further he simply got Jack to agree to come to the bank tomorrow before he opened the bar so they could have a little parlay "man to man." Jack virtually fled back behind the bar and busied himself washing glasses and tidying up until the men left for their dinners at home. But part of him was proud. A legislator…imagine that.

14.

Eventually Jack ran into Wild Bill, Jake and the other member of their team, Lefty Louie, so named because he was missing his left hand, the unfortunate result of being caught cheating at cards. "Hey, where's your bear?" WB started in kidding Jack. "Still puttin' on them fights?"

Jack was immediately offended. He had begun to see himself as a statesman already. "I'll have you know I'll be running for a seat in the new legislature," he huffed. "The bankers here and the other powers that be seem to think I have the right stuff for it."

At the mention of bankers, the gears started turning in WB's head. He and his cohorts had fixed a few elections back East and here might be the opportunity to do so again. "So, they're paying you to run, is that it?"

Clearly offended, Jack snapped, "Nothing of the sort! They're just encouraging me and being the influential men they are, I'm sure the voters will see it in their best interest." Jack rarely ever made a speech even that long, but he didn't want it out about his past life. "I talked to the sheriff the other day about you boys," he added, "and I think you best be moving along, maybe go on down to Reno, or even San Francisco."

"Well, that's not a very friendly way to be to your old friends," WB laughed. "Why we might even be able to campaign for you, you know, help you win that there election." Jake had already caught on to the scheme and pulled Louie aside, explaining how they might soon be meeting with the bankers themselves and getting a little money to ensure the voters were of a like mind. "I'm thinkin' we could do a little persuading, you might say, so's folks wouldn't even consider another candidate."

Jack knew just how they operated and finally pulled WB up by his coat lapels. "You'll do nothing of the sort. I don't need a thug like you, or your friends," and he glared at Louie, "persuading anyone to do anything for me." He shoved WB back into his seat and added, "In fact, I believe I'll be persuading the sheriff to put you on tonight's train."

Louie and Jake both stood but then recalled the beatings they had seen Jack dish out. "Oh come on, Jack, we're just funnin' with you." Jake pulled on WB's arm and said, "Yeah, we were just saying this town's too small for our kind of operation, weren't we, WB?" WB glowered at his men and at Jack but finally stood slowly and doffed his hat to Jack.

"All success, Jack, old friend, all success." He and the others were almost to the door of the saloon, however, when he couldn't resist getting in a final shot. "And when you go home tonight, you give our regards to that old bear."

Jack was riled enough to head on down to the Delta for a whiskey or two, maybe even a poke with one of the whores. When he pushed through the doors of the saloon he was surprised to see his old piano-playing friend Philip sitting at the old upright plinking out a tune. "Say there, this is a surprise! San Francisco run you out?"

Philip immediately jumped up to shake Jack's hand. "I thought you might be too good for a place like this," he said bowing deeply to him, "beings how you're about to be governor or some such exalted personage." The two men turned to the bar and Philip continued, "No, I did a bit of work for Juliette, actually." Jack raised an eyebrow to the young man. "She rounded up some new whores and wanted me to escort them up here for her." He lowered his voice and leaned toward Jack. "And boy, are they something! Virginia City's never seen the likes."

Jack swiveled around to look at the balcony over the saloon but saw no one new. "So, what arc they all taken already?"

"No, Juliette's teachin' them the ropes, I reckon."

Jack put the whores out of his mind for a moment and turned back to Philip. "And how's your bride and the baby?"

Philip immediately looked downcast and Jack regretted his inquiry. "She's been pretty unhappy, to tell the truth. She didn't want the baby and now that he's here, she's even worse."

"It's a boy then. Well, congratulations!" Jack said heartily, but he could see Philip just deflected the comment.

"He's Padraig's son all right. I didn't think it would pain me but it does." He described the arrangement with Fiona taking all responsibility for the baby and Kathleen ignoring all three of them. "I love San Francisco and Mr. Mackay lined me up with a great job, but to tell the truth, I don't even want to go back there."

Jack was shocked and saddened for his friend. "Well, you can't be talking like that. You've got responsibilities and you've got to be a man and live up to them."

Philip was chastened and just replied quietly. "I know. I know I do." Little did Philip know, however, how things were changing in San Francisco.

15.

The baby simply would not stop coughing. Fiona gave Patrick a sugar cloth to suck on and rocked him endlessly but he coughed and gasped until he was nearly blue. Kathleen grew more and more exasperated but could think of nothing to do that would help, finally just shutting herself in her room. When Philip had left a week earlier she barely acknowledged him, thinking she would like to have been the one escorting the new whores to Virginia City and admitting it would be unlikely that she would return. Now she wondered, would he return? She certainly hadn't been much of a wife to him, and he was even less interested in the baby than she was.

Kathleen knew Fiona had stars in her eyes when it came to Philip and especially to the baby, and there were times when she wanted to say, "Oh, just take the both of them and leave me be!" She had to continually remind herself that Fiona had been a godsend; certainly neither she nor the baby would probably even be alive without her.

Two days later the baby was no better and Fiona was beginning to show signs of exhaustion herself. Kathleen finally had to insist that they take the baby to a doctor, so for once she took charge of getting the baby ready, helping Fiona put on a clean dress, and fixing her own hair and dress. After the baby's birth they had gone to the local doctor for a checkup where Patrick was pronounced fit as a fiddle, but when the carriage pulled up in front of the doctor's storefront this time, they were amazed to see women and children lined up on the street.

"What's going on?" Kathleen asked the coachman.

"Oh, ma'am, it's the diphtheria, they say it's broke out all across the city," he explained and gave the horses a quick swat of his whip, anxious to get away from the crowd of sick people.

"Diphtheria?" Kathleen turned to Fiona who now looked quite ill. "Do you suppose we should stay or go back home?" Fiona was too weak to even answer, but just then a mother and infant came out of the office.

"Take the night airs! That's all he has to say, like it's the croup!" The mother began to cry and hurried off with her baby.

"I think we should go," Kathleen said, taking Fiona's arm. But just as they stepped into the line waiting for carriages, Fiona collapsed on the street. Kathleen caught Patrick as Fiona fell, Patrick crying and coughing all the louder. The doctor came out of the clinic, having been alerted by some of the other patients waiting in line. He took one look at Fiona and yelled for his staff to bring a stretcher and ferry her to the hospital. Kathleen was stunned, but then the doctor grabbed Patrick as well. "And send her baby with her!" he commanded. She started to explain that she was Patrick's mother but he had already moved on to other agitated women and children.

That night she prayed for Fiona and for Patrick, something she hadn't done in a long time. She wished Philip were home. She wished she was still in the safety of Emma's rooms in Virginia City. When she went to the hospital the next morning she got the news she had half-dreaded and half-expected. Both Fiona and Patrick had died in the night.

Kathleen walked the streets aimlessly for most of the day but finally went back to the little house on Russian Hill where she composed a note to Philip. "The baby took sick, and then Fiona as well. Both were rushed to the hospital but both passed. I'm sorry for your loss." She thought about crossing out 'your' and substituting 'our' but thought the meaning was clear enough. She then packed a few of her belongings, set the note on the dining table, and left for the shipyards, determined to return forever to Ireland.

16.

Vicente stewed about Juliette and whether he should offer her the chance at immortality. He wondered whether he would be doing it for his own selfish reasons, to have a companion for eons to come. Was she sophisticated and worldly enough for his tastes or would she insist on staying in Virginia City until the silver ran out completely? He made himself stay away from her many nights in a row but always found himself at the foot of the stairs in the Delta. The other whores, thinking him rich, were always trying to rub up against him or entice him in other small ways, but it was only Juliette that drew him.

Finally, when she emerged one evening in a black velvet gown with a diamond choker (a gift from another admirer!), Vicente could wait no longer. He sat on the edge of her bed and proclaimed, "You know I can give you everything you desire, life and fame immortal." When she didn't respond immediately, he plunged on. "With just the tiniest little bite on the neck, it could all be yours." Subtlety was not his strong suit.

"You're brushed my hair, you've washed my feet, and now you want to bite me on the neck?" Juliette laughed. "Well, go ahead, it's no more than others have done before you," and she leaned forward, tugging the choker down.

His pride was momentarily offended. "Well, actually it is much, much, much more than others have done before!" At this he bared his fangs, the first time ever in polite company. "I offer you the chance to live on forever, just as you are tonight (and here he thought, why didn't I shave her legs when I had the chance?)."

"Oh, I expect I'm getting well-known enough to live on forever whether you bite me or not," Juliette said petulantly. "After all, I'm the one that invented the washing up, and I'm the one that brought these exotic Asian whores here, and I'm the one that…"

"Oh stop it!" Vicente was growing increasingly frustrated with this object of his desires. "Have you never heard of the kiss of the immortals?" Seeing her bewildered look, he continued. "Vampires? Ring any bells?"

Of course, she had read about such things but always believed them to be no more than fantasies. But here he stood before her. If he truly was a vampire, it would go a long way toward explaining his many peculiarities. She had often imagined living into the next century or beyond, but she also questioned whether her imagination was a curse or a blessing. The things she could dream up! Still Vicente waited, and finally Juliette had to answer him. "I expect in the future a whole class of people will be famous just for being famous, and I also expect I don't need to lead such a fatuous existence." She could match his vocabulary any day with all the reading she had done.

"But I could take you to Europe, show you the great cities of the world," he pleaded, noting her complexion suddenly shift from light pink to green (she recalling the boat trip, of course). "We would want for nothing! The world would be our oyster."

"Oh, I had those in San Francisco, slimy little things," Juliette said with a dismissive wave of her hand. "No, no more oysters for this girl. Give me a bloody steak any day."

Just as she said 'bloody' Vicente's frustration and impatience boiled over, but there was a knock on the door. "Come in," she called out lightly, ignoring Vicente's burning countenance entirely.

In walked the most exquisite creature Vicente had seen in ages…and ages and ages. He took in the long manicured hands and tapered fingernails with perhaps just a hint of polish, the wavy blonde hair, and the long slender neck, and it was just too much to bear. Even vampires have needs, he reconciled to himself, as he threw himself on the hapless pianist. Oh! It was just this sort of impetuous action that had gotten him banished before, but he truly, truly couldn't help himself. He gathered Philip in his arms and with just one glance back at Juliette, fled into the night. He would explain things later.

After they left, Juliette had very little time to dwell on such a curious event. The girls she had imported from the Far East via San Francisco had brought with them cholera. Their customers were sickened and died, as did Juliette herself despite the ministrations of the city's best physicians.

Jack spoke at her funeral and said she would indeed take her place in history. He talked about her untamed spirit, something he thought about again when he was later sworn into the legislature, looking at the Great Seal of the State of Nevada and wondering why it didn't depict the mustang, what he considered the ultimate symbol of freedom and life.

Book Three

Watched Over...

1.

Vicente was extremely ashamed of himself for inflicting the Kiss of the Immortals on Philip. He told himself he would never, never, never bestow the gift — or the punishment — on anyone without their being a willing participant. But, he was just so *frustrated* over that silly wench, Juliette, that he couldn't stop himself when he saw Philip's lustrous blonde locks and long alabaster neck. It didn't help matters that Philip had just played a concert and was still wearing his lovely maroon velvet jacket and matching paisley cravat. Well, really, when you looked at it in just that light it was hardly Vicente's fault at all!

The actual event was somewhat of a blur in Vicente's mind as it all transpired so quickly. He knew that Juliette had fainted when she saw Vicente force himself on Philip, so that was a good thing. Maybe she would convince herself that she had seen something entirely different. There were always men who preferred men after all, she would tell herself. She would congratulate herself on not falling for Vicente's various charms, and in months to come she would probably brag to the other whores about her superior understanding of men. Yes, he could see exactly that scenario unfolding. He would be laughed about and scorned! Oh, of course, she would just *have* to tell them all about how he wanted to do nothing more than brush her hair or wash her feet. The vision of that singular experience made him shudder anew. He had actually entertained thoughts of sending her a lovely women's razor with a gentle note, all very delicately wrapped with a fresh gardenia on top, perhaps. But no, there was no point in that now.

After the unfortunate…event…Vicente had spirited Philip's limp body back to the tunnels and to his own resting chamber, gently ministering to him when he finally awoke. Curiously, Philip was not so much frightened as he was intrigued. He seemed to sense immediately that he had undergone a great change, although he was at a loss to define it. Vicente was still reluctant to explain what had befallen the young pianist and that he, Vicente, was responsible. When Philip finally felt well enough to leave the tunnels, Vicente was at last forced to tell him the truth. Fortunately, Vicente prided himself on being a master of words in virtually any language. Still, he stammered. "Actually, you can't go out just now," he told Philip, gently brushing some rock dust from his jacket. "It's uh, well, dangerous."

Philip nearly mocked him. "Dangerous? Are there mountain lions in the vicinity? Perhaps rattlers? Rustlers? Hucksters? Just what could be so dangerous?" he taunted Vicente, while at the same time flexing what he felt was a new strength. "We're not afraid of the rough miners with their nasty picks and shovels are we?" he leered.

"No, it's the sun, you smart-ass!" Vicente snapped. "I've made you a vampire and you can no longer go out in the sunlight. It's as simple as that. Unless, of course, you want to burst into flames!" He had hoped to make a more gradual, eloquent explanation of the whole affair, but Philip had forced his hand.

"You've made me a *what*?" Philip asked, clearly stunned. His cockiness evaporated as quickly as the morning dew.

"Now, really it's not as bad as all that," Vicente rushed to soothe him. "You're just not going to be a morning person any longer, but you will own the night." He could see that he wasn't getting through to the young man. "Please, just let me explain this in the right way."

"Oh, there's a right way, is there, to be told you've become some sort of monster!" Philip erupted.

Now it was Vicente's turn to be upset. "I resent that, young man! I am no monster, as you can plainly see, and you shall be lucky indeed to turn out half as well as myself." He brushed away a rock and motioned Philip to sit, to which his young protégé reluctantly acquiesced. "There are certain basics and you will have to learn them, just as you learned the scales on the piano from your mother."

Again, Philip's indignation flared. "I'll not have you mentioning my mother in such a horrible circumstance."

"Tut, tut. It was just an analogy, if you'll indulge me." Seeing Philip gradually begin to settle again, Vicente continued. "Now, what would be horrible would be to burst into flames. Just let me mention that again. You simply cannot ever, ever go out into the sunlight. You must be back in your chambers by dawn and you cannot leave again until the sun is well below the horizon." Vicente stood with his hands clasped behind his back, waiting for some acknowledgement from his new pupil.

"But what about…" Philip's question died on his lips.

"Yes, there are things that you must sacrifice, but also much that you may gain," Vicente said promisingly. "Let us rest now and when the moon rises tonight, I will take you out and begin to show you your new life." Vicente hoped he was smiling when he said this, but at the same time he felt very much saddened and turned to hide his expression from Philip. For his part, Philip said nothing and also turned away, hoping Vicente would not see his expression either.

2.

But when the moon rose that night, they did not go out. Vicente correctly assumed that Philip was still too vulnerable and too unstable to simply reappear in polite society. For that night and many to come, Vicente assumed the role of teacher and mentor, painstakingly imparting the strengths and weaknesses of being a vampire. He suffered Philip's endless interruptions, pleas, threats and even insults with equanimity; it was, after all, his fault they were sitting in a dank cave rather than at the Opera House or with the convivial group at the Delta.

"Why is all this instruction of yours taking so long?" Philip demanded over and over again. "I just feel I'll go straight out of my mind with another night in this cave."

"Oh hush! Rome wasn't built in a day, and I should know because I was there to see it!" Vicente managed to mask his exasperation with his new pupil, but there were times when it was almost too much.

"Why can't we go out to eat?" Philip whined.

"We can't go out to eat because we don't eat, you ninny." He had gone over the whole issue of no longer needing food or wine, or even water, a dozen times already. "Are you hungry, or are you just whining to try my patience?"

Philip looked abashed for a moment, but then had to press the issue. "But surely we need some…nourishment?"

Vicente knew were Philip was headed with his question. "Perhaps you've read too many Victorian novels, my dear friend." Philip fixed him with a malevolent stare. "Well, all right. Of course, you're correct. At least initially you will need some…nourishment." Philip continued to glare at Vicente, obliging him to continue. "In time, these needs can be controlled and even completely sublimated. In time." Vicente hoped that would end the discussion, but Philip pressed him.

"In time? Time? A week, a month, a year, how long?" he implored the elder vampire.

"Well, over the long run…" but Philip immediately interrupted him with a threatening slice of his hand and another venomous gaze. "For me it was, oh, I forget, sixty years, seventy, something like that, really not too long at all," Vicente replied gaily.

"In seventy years I'll be dead," Philip huffed.

"Have you been listening to a thing I've said?" Vicente was riled. "You'll never be dead, never, hence the name, the undead!" Vicente had been hoping it wouldn't have come to this juncture so soon, but it was clear he would have to address the key issue much sooner than later. "Haven't you noticed how cool your own skin is becoming? I saw you trying to cut yourself on a rock. Nothing happened did it?" Vicente drew quite close to Philip. "Have you had any thoughts of sex? Any ability to carry it out?" Philip shrank back, but Vicente pushed forward. "Of course not. We no longer have any blood in our veins. I'm sure you can figure out what that does for the plumbing." Philip looked quite downcast by now, but Vicente wasn't ready to end the lesson. "Without blood in our veins, we are cold, cold people."

But now Philip saw the essential question. "But are we people at all?"

3.

"You might see yourself as a monster," Vicente accused Philip, "but I refuse to. I have all the humanity I ever had. I care, I tell you, I care." They went to their respective sleeping chambers quite angry with each other, but as the sun sank the next evening, Vicente realized there was no point in postponing the inevitable.

When at last they did emerge from the mine tunnel, they naturally drifted toward the Delta saloon, although along the way Philip had some business to address. Part of Philip's education from Vicente had been how to select his victims and how to take their lives with a certain amount of reverence. Now it was time to see if Philip had paid attention to Vicente's strict dictums: No young people in the prime of their lives, no obviously diseased people, no pregnant or nursing women, no children, and the list went on. In exasperation, Philip asked, "Am I only to seek volunteers?" And he couldn't resist adding, "I was in the prime of *my* life when you chose *me*!" Vicente couldn't get him to see the difference between the Kiss of the Immortal and the drink of death.

Finally they came across a man of perhaps 40 years of age who had stepped into an alleyway to relieve himself. "Quickly, do it now!" Vicente urged. Philip leapt on the man and did as Vicente had shown him. The whole act was over in a minute and the man's crumpled body lay sprawled in the alley. Vicente took a moment to pull the man out of the mud and prop him up against the shack, looking for all the world like he was perhaps sleeping off a drunken evening. "No sense leaving a mess for someone else to find," he lectured Philip quite primly. Vicente was quite disappointed to see Philip giddy with excitement rather than somber and respectful, but he knew that phase would eventually pass, as it had with him as well.

They had made up their minds to tell anyone who asked that Philip had been on tour with an opera company, accounting for his absence. But, they needn't have bothered. The mood in the Delta was somber indeed. Jack sat at a corner table with some of his political cronies but even they conversed listlessly. The piano lid was closed and black bunting hung from the balcony where normally the whores would have been on display. Vicente looked up the staircase hopefully, but it was Jack who broke the news. "She won't never be coming down those stairs again," he intoned. "She's left us."

"Left?" Vicente stammered. "To go where?" Part of his brain knew the answer, but he had to hear it out loud.

"The cholera took her. She's dead now two weeks come Thursday," Jack said softly. After all, she was his love, too. "The whores have scrubbed the place top to bottom, but no one feels much like working."

Vicente noticed the whores gathered at another table, the announcement setting off another round of crying among them. As they dabbed their eyes with handkerchiefs, it was plain that their fingers were rough and reddened.

"Where is she?" Vicente inquired gently.

"Down the hill in the graveyard," Jack replied. "Damn near the whole town turned out for the funeral." He started to choke up but continued with more details. "The Clampers and the firemen especially did right by her. You'll see how nice her grave is," and he hesitated, "assuming you're going to go down there?"

Vicente was bereft, but of course, no tear could fall. "Yes, I must go." He felt he could tear his hair out from grief, but it would be a pointless gesture at best; the hair would be fully restored the next evening as, of course, he would never age. He stumbled out of the Delta and made his way down the hill. Indeed, Juliette's grave was lovely. A short wrought-iron fence set it off from the others in a delicate pattern of vines interspersed with little bells that tinkled in the breeze. A pale pink granite slab was inscribed in a flowing cursive script:

Juliette Wells

The Belle of Virginia City
A comfort to all who knew her

Even in his anguish Vicente recognized the irony in that tribute and felt it wouldn't be long before some jealous wife would deface the marker. He moved a tall arrangement of flowers to conceal it. "Oh, you silly, wonderful woman," Vicente said, kneeling before the grave. "Why couldn't you have accepted the gift I had to bestow?" He prostrated himself before the headstone. "The places we would have seen!" He thought of all the gowns he had imagined her wearing, a lavender tulle for a midnight stroll through the gardens of Versailles, a crushed green velvet to attend the opera in London, a saucy red lace frock to prowl the trattorias of Rome. Completely lost in his musings, Vicente nearly missed the first rays of the sun. He realized he must quickly return to the tunnels and hoped Philip would already be there. He had quite forgotten about him in his grief.

4.

Philip was stunned by the news of Juliette's passing and did the only thing he could think of to do—he opened the piano and began to play hymns he had learned as a child. A few of whores, and eventually even the miners, sung along. Philip certainly did feel like a hypocrite, however, playing "Nearer My God to Thee," when he was certain that his new 'condition' rendered him an abomination in God's eyes. But the old hymns did seem comforting and at the same time lifted the mood in the Delta, drinks flowed more freely and the whores acknowledged that perhaps they could do a poke or two. One of the new young girls approached Philip with just such an offer. "Hey, candy man," she cooed in his ear, "let me do something nice for you tonight like you just done for us." But when her lips touched his neck, she drew back. "Honey, you're a block of ice!" He brushed her aside, mumbling some excuse about not feeling well and immediately left the Delta.

He gradually wandered the darkened streets up to The Corner Saloon which had been rebuilt after the great fire, although the actual opera house was lagging behind in the construction effort. First things first, Philip mused, gazing in the windows at the usual crowd of mine owners and bankers. Even though he knew he would have been welcomed, he couldn't force himself to go in and instead turned back down the hill, making his way back to the tunnels. The sadness he felt at Juliette's passing followed him back to the cave and for a moment he thought about just finding a place atop one of the hills to welcome the sunrise and his death. But Philip had responsibilities, and these weighed on him just as heavily as his sadness. He settled in the tunnel and awaited Vicente's return.

Indeed, Vicente was much surprised to find Philip already in their hideaway beneath the mountain. His acolyte looked pensive, so Vicente said nothing as they retired to their respective sleeping quarters, each to dream about a love that was lost.

The next evening, Philip was blunt. "I will be leaving for San Francisco as soon as I can make the appropriate travel arrangements, and I expect you to help me do so."

Vicente was not totally surprised but he still felt the need to protest. "But, you're not ready to be out on your own. It's just too soon." He added, "There are so many things left for me to teach you."

But the piano player would not be dissuaded. "I have a wife and a child, and I am still responsible for them."

Vicente's mind was racing (as it often was). "I'm telling you in no uncertain terms that you, a fledgling vampire at best, are *not* strong enough to make Kathleen one of us!"

Philip was aghast. "The thought had never crossed my mind!" He pointed his finger in Vicente's chest. "Why on earth would you think I would want anyone I loved to become this, this…thing?" He had to turn his back on Vicente so as not to see the look of disappointment on the elder's face. "I am simply telling you that provisions for their future have to be made. I am her husband and that is all there is to it." And seconds later, "And, you know, there is the baby to think of, too." Vicente realized there was no stopping Philip and over the next few hours they made arrangements for his safe transport to San Francisco, much as Vicente had traveled there several times.

If Philip was reluctant to think about the baby, Kathleen was as well. She tortured herself with the question of whether she missed the baby or not. She couldn't even think of it as *her* baby; it was just *the* baby. It may have been her own flesh and blood, but conceived in violence as it was, she doubted the maternal-child bond would ever have developed. In the weeks since the baby's and Fiona's deaths, Kathleen had taken to walking about the house in her stocking feet. Even the sound of her shoes on the wood floors seemed too much. Where the view of the harbor had once comforted her, now it was all she could do to look out the window. She knew this was no longer her home, if it ever had been. She missed Philip, or at least she missed the Philip of the Opera House days, but she found herself strangely detached from the idea of him returning to the city by the Bay. She couldn't picture doing even the simplest things with him, sharing a meal, taking a walk in the park, much less reigniting their passion for each other.

Finally, she knew what had to be done. Taking pen to paper, she began the note to him. "Dearest Philip. I am sorry not to be here to greet you, and I hope your travels were not too tiring." She thought about tearing up the note then, but she steeled herself to continue. "Little Patrick and dear Fiona have passed due to the whooping cough that raged through the city. I myself was unaffected." Truly? "I have realized that San Francisco will never be home to me, perhaps America itself was not my destiny. I plan to seek passage on a steamer bound for Ireland and hope to leave on the morrow. I am using the money you put aside for the baby and hope that in the future I may find a way to repay your kindness." Kathleen knew the note did not address their marital relationship. "I loved you dearly and will always carry you in my heart, but I could never have been the wife you truly deserved—and one I hope you will find, with my blessings." How to sign it? "Yours, Kathleen." But, of course, she no longer would be his. "Love?" On some level. Finally she settled for, "With deepest affection and esteem, Kathleen." She placed the note against the teapot in the center of the dining table and went to her room to pack her steamer trunk.

5.

Kathleen enjoyed the voyage round the Horn and back to Ireland. She was snug in her own private cabin, albeit a small one with only a tiny porthole, the memories of her previous journey in steerage largely faded. She was not the type to ruminate on the past and wonder what she had done to deserve the various fates that had already befallen her. Instead, she thought only of the future and she used the long sailing to work out the details of her plans. Initially she had thought about returning to the village of her birth, but again, there would be nothing but sad memories, so she dismissed the idea. She yearned to be among Irish people again, but not those rooted so deeply in the past that they failed to see the future ahead of them. She took stock of her limited skills and realized that her time working with the wardrobe mistress in the Opera House had given her a unique exposure to a colorful part of society bursting with vitality — the theater world, of course.

The more Kathleen thought about her life, the more resolute she became. She was still a young woman after all, even though twice married, widowed and having lost a child. She was young and she could — and would — have young thoughts, ideas and a life again. She immediately began sketching elaborate costumes which she knew she was capable of making. The Dublin Opera Company was new, but even Philip had talked about them and said critics deemed them worthy of a bright future that would attract increasingly better and better talent. Kathleen resolved to be part of that talent, although thinking about Philip's delight in music gave her a pang of sadness. Yes, she would create costumes that would make even the most pedestrian singer seem glamorous and enchanting! If even one diva wore a creation by Kathleen, soon other performers would want them. Her dreams and imagination soared.

At nearly the same time Kathleen had her inspiration, Philip stood in the little house in San Francisco reading her letter to him. He was shocked to hear about the baby and Fiona, although not as sad as he might have been, perhaps a manifestation of his new state, he wondered briefly. He also had a hard time defining the emotion he felt at Kathleen's abandonment, which was truly how he saw it. He paced the floors becoming more indignant by the moment. Why here he had married her knowing she was pregnant with another man's child and had promised to raise and care for that child! And she just leaves him with a pithy note! "Deepest affection," my ass, he thought. Was she just an opportunist who had used him to get that much closer to a harbor and from there back to Ireland? He tortured himself until nearly sunup with questions about every plan they had ever made or dream they had shared. Had any of it ever been true? He finally locked himself in the small dark bedroom and slept the day away.

When Philip awakened that night it was with fresh resolve to find Kathleen and confront her about her intentions and their life together. She had said she would be leaving on a steamer the day after she wrote the note, which must mean she would be taking the long way around the Horn and back to the continent. He could get there first. He would be standing on the dock when she arrived (provided it was at night, damn it, he thought) and judge by the look on her face whether she had truly abandoned him or just fled without thinking. He would return to Virginia City immediately and enlist Vicente's help in his plan. He had to return in any event since he had borrowed Vicente's splendid black cloaked carriage for the trip to San Francisco.

He climbed into the carriage that night and gave the coachman strict instructions not to disturb him until they had entered Virginia City at dusk a few days hence. But as soon as he drew the heavy velvet curtains, he could hear Vicente's voice mocking him. "Oh, certainly, just see her and explain everything. You could clasp her to your cold, hard breast and what?" Philip didn't have an answer just yet but by the time he arrived in Virginia City to endure Vicente's questioning, he would. At least he hoped he would.

6.

Vicente idly wondered what progress Philip was making with Kathleen, although he knew the whole venture was doomed from the start. Kathleen could not be expected to simply accept Philip as a vampire and Philip would be heartbroken at her rejection. Vicente just hoped Philip didn't do anything rash as young vampires often did (he himself, of course, but he preferred not to think of that time).

In the meantime, Vicente found himself increasingly drawn to Jack, the bartender turned statesman. They sat in the Delta one evening, both looking toward the balcony. "You know, she was like an angel my wife had sent," Jack said. "Odd thing to say about a whore, I know, but that's how I felt, like my wife was just up there watching over me."

Vicente nodded and chose his words carefully. "You know, I loved her in my own way, but she was just like those mustangs you're so fond of. No one would tame her, I suspect." Jack finished off a shot of whiskey while Vicente knocked the ash off the end of his cigar. Although Vicente was well past the pleasures of the flesh, he found that he simply *loved* to smoke. He loved holding the cigar, and in the tunnel in private, he practiced his best pose with it — right hand or left? He adored the little ritual of cutting off one end, then licking the other before lighting it. Often Jack or one of the whores would offer the burning match, and Vicente loved looking into their eyes as the cigar caught the flame. Cigarettes just didn't have the same cache as cigars, Vicente thought, and there was that whole mess of having to roll them yourself.

Oh, and that first puff, puff, puff getting it started. It was a lot like kissing that young girl in the woods years and years ago. Then, the first deep draw of smoke down into his lungs, so very satisfying. And it was amusing as well. He found he could blow out spectacular circles of smoke, sometimes circles within circles. He had not found anything nearly as pleasing in hundreds of years. He lovingly prolonged the last inhalation of the night, waiting in his cave for the sun's early rays, and when he awoke the next night it was with anticipation of his next cigar and the lovely spiraling tendrils of smoke.

Yes, indeed, Vicente felt there were many benefits of smoking, not the least of which it allowed him to spend time in polite company without being overly questioned about his not drinking. "One vice at a time," he would joke with the whores and the miners, "one vice at a time." He suspected Jack had his doubts, but if he did he kept them to himself, although one night he surprised Vicente with an odd observation.

"You're an old soul, ain't you?"

Now what could he mean by *that*, Vicente wondered, but he answered thoughtfully. "I suppose people think that because I'm rather serious about life (now there's a laugh)."

"No, there's more to it than that, but it's your business," Jack allowed and looked at the other man quite directly. "I just say live and let live," and the two left the conversation at that, both a little wary of the other.

The arrival of Vicente's coach outside the saloon provided the perfect distraction from the tense moment. Philip burst into the saloon and sunk into a chair with the others. "Kathleen's left me. The baby's dead. The nanny is dead."

Vicente leaned forward, "You didn't…"

"No, you fool. They were gone when I got there. The diphtheria killed the baby and Fiona and then Kathleen just up and left, said she was getting on a steamer back to Ireland." He showed Vicente and Jack the note, even though he was humiliated by its less than passionate contents.

"Well, women take things like that hard," Jack offered.

Vicente had seen how ambivalent Kathleen had been about the pregnancy, so he doubted Jack was correct, but he shook his head in agreement. "I suppose when she gets back home she'll be happier. I don't believe she had a happy moment here," and he rushed to add, "although I know you tried, Philip, you truly did."

Philip put his head in his hands. "I can't let her go like that. I'd always wonder if it was me she didn't want or just what all."

The three men sat quietly, but Vicente already had a foreboding about where this would lead. It would be time for a long talk when they returned to their lair in the tunnels.

7.

As Kathleen's ship progressed down the coast of the South American continent, virtually every port seemed to entice her deeper into her dreams. These were not the bustling seaports of Boston or New York, or even St. Louis, but small trading posts where local natives met the ships and exchanged whatever goods they had for supplies not available in the South American jungles. While it was nice to be on solid land for a few hours at each stop, it was these wharfside marketplaces that enthralled Kathleen. Natives offered a spectacular bounty of handmade crafts with designs she had never seen before. The intricate weavings, not only of cloth, but of baskets, captured her sensibilities as a seamstress and inspired her as an artist. Not only that, there were always baskets of exotic feathers on display as well as beads made from materials Kathleen couldn't even guess. She saw them decorating the gowns of Europe's biggest opera stars and stage actresses. She could hardly tear herself away when the ship's whistle blew, signaling the time for sailing, and would immediately go back to her cabin to begin sketching her latest inspirations.

Although Kathleen and most of the other passengers dreaded the actual 'rounding of the Horn,' fearing its legendary rough seas, there were days and days of smooth sailing and the crew did their best to ensure everyone's comfort. The highlight of the cruise for many was when the ship crossed the equator. Most of the sailors had done it before and had crude tattoos commemorating the event, but they still put on quite a lively party for the guests with skits, music and dancing that went on till the early morning hours. Kathleen even rigged up a few costumes so the rough sailors could play the parts of native women, much to everyone's delight.

After a particularly ribald skit, Kathleen found herself laughing out loud, then stopped, much ashamed of herself. She was, after all, only a month past losing her child and leaving her husband. But when the sailor playing a giant monkey beat his chest and another sailor with a blonde wig swooned and allowed 'herself' to be carried off into the jungle, Kathleen began laughing again, and this time wholeheartedly. There was no point in waiting for happiness, even momentary, when it was right in front of her.

At the same time, there was no happiness awaiting Philip in the tunnels beneath Virginia City. He and Vicente had argued long into the night, on more than one night, about Philip's plan to race across the country and board a ship in New York, thereby arriving in Dublin before Kathleen. He would then confront her with her abandonment of him, and then…and this is where Vicente always questioned, "And then what?" Philip had no answer. Vicente waited patiently, blowing those damnable smoke rings. "Oooh, look, that one looks just like a seahorse!" Philip had never seen a seahorse, of course, and couldn't understand Vicente's newfound obsession with smoking.

Philip stayed in his own section of the deep mine tunnels for weeks, alternately disconsolate, frustrated and angry, more frustrated than anything though. He had loved Kathleen, truly, and had done something few men would in marrying her even knowing she was pregnant with another man's child. He had fully expected to raise the child and be with Kathleen long into old age. At times he blamed Vicente. How could he possibly have any relationship with Kathleen thanks to what Vicente had done! At other times he blamed Kathleen. She couldn't have waited to tell him in person about the baby and her own desire to return to Ireland! And he blamed himself. Why did he drag her to a city she plainly didn't care for just so he could pursue his own career! He felt like a dog chasing its tail, if not this, that; if not that, this.

But Philip was finally saved from his downward spiral when Vicente rushed into the cave one night with exciting news. The greatest opera singer of the day was coming to Virginia City and would perform at the Opera House six weeks hence! "You must dust yourself off," Vicente lectured Philip while quite literally brushing the dust off his jacket, "and get down to the Opera House, tell them you will be ready to accompany the star."

"The Opera House hasn't even been rebuilt," Philip scoffed. "Is he going to sing in The Corner Saloon, then?"

"Oh, you petulant boy!" Vicente exclaimed in exasperation. "While you've been here wallowing in self-pity, the town has positively rallied behind the completion of the Opera House. Why just this evening they were putting in rows of velvet-seated chairs." He went on for some minutes describing the grandeur of the newly-rebuilt hall but could see Philip plainly ignoring him. He had saved the best for last, however.

"Tomorrow they will uncrate the new Steinway. I wonder who they'll get to tune it…"

At this Philip perked up somewhat but refused to show any excitement. "Oh, I suppose old Bill from the Washoe Club. He thinks he's a pianist all right." He scuffed the toe of his boot in the dirt. "I don't imagine anyone has missed me, after all."

Vicente wanted to burst out laughing but restrained himself in kindness to his young friend. "Oh, your name comes up every night when some clodhopper begins banging away on that rickety old piano in the Delta." He added slyly, "Yes, they all say only Philip could make even that thing truly sing." When Philip failed to respond Vicente played his hole card. "Apparently one of the supper clubs in San Francisco said they could loan their pianist for a few nights, someone who was hired to replace you, in fact."

"They couldn't replace me that easily," Philip huffed. "We'll just see who will play for the big opera star!"

8.

A young woman traveling alone naturally attracted a certain amount of attention, and not just among the sailors. For that reason Kathleen took most of her meals in her cabin, although occasionally the captain requested that everyone join him for the evening meal. He used these occasions to give impromptu talks about the ports they would be visiting, the expected weather they might encounter, and the nature of the people who lived near the ports. Kathleen was relieved that she had made herself a couple of dress and coat combinations for nights out in San Francisco that were perfectly serviceable for these dinners. Still, she sat alone or with another older woman and excused herself at the earliest possible opportunity without seeming rude.

On one such occasion, however, a note was delivered to her cabin in the early afternoon. "Will the lady please do us the honor of joining our table for dinner? If you would like, we could meet in the salon beforehand for a sherry." It was signed Arthur and Vivian McDougall. Kathleen had no idea who they were and the deckhand who had delivered the note spoke no English. She nearly laughed with the vision of herself entering the salon and confronting every couple there. "Sherry? No? Sherry? No?" Of course, they knew *her*, so she was just being silly. She debated with herself but in the end realized there was simply no avoiding it unless she wanted to miss the dinner entirely. She would wear her best dress and enter the salon head held high.

At the appointed hour Kathleen did just that and was immediately approached by a very distinguished-looking older gentleman who bowed before her, kissed her gloved hand and introduced himself. "Arthur McDougall, and that is my sister, just there," he pointed to a woman perhaps in her fifties, "Vivian. We're so glad you decided to join us this evening."

"Your invitation is most kind," Kathleen half-curtsied. "I am Kathleen Evans." She winced at the use of Philip's last name; she had barely gotten used to being Kathleen Kelly when Padraig died and couldn't think when she had ever introduced herself as Evans unless it was at the doctor's office. Arthur steered her to where Vivian was seated and the introductions were repeated. A decanter of sherry sat on the table with three crystal glasses which Arthur immediately filled.

"A toast then, to the spirit of adventure and to travelers everywhere. May they always find welcome," Arthur intoned while the three clinked their glasses together. "Now then, mysterious Miss Evans, what brings you aboard this vessel?"

"Well, I'm returning home to Ireland," Kathleen replied hesitantly.

"Yes, yes, that is the *boat's* destination," Arthur responded, then teasing her, "but what is *your* destination?"

Kathleen was flustered but plunged in. "I am a costume designer for the stage, and an opportunity has presented itself for me to design for the Dublin Opera."

"Ah, just so," Arthur nodded. "You do have a certain style. Vivian said the same when she first saw you, isn't that right, Vivian?" Getting no response from his sister, Arthur continued his interrogation. "So, you have designed for other companies, other playhouses, I take it?"

Kathleen knew she was trapped. "Yes, I, uh…" She took a sip of the sweet sherry. "I worked in San Francisco most recently at the California Theater. Perhaps you know it?" Arthur refilled his glass and encouraged her to continue. "Yes, Mr. Ralston of the Bank of California built it, and it is so grand inside with murals of the city." Kathleen warmed to her own description. She recalled the afternoon Philip had taken her to see the empty theater while he applied for a job in their orchestra. "They, I mean we, just presented 'Money' and it was quite successful."

The steward rang the bell signaling guests to enter the dining room. Arthur helped first his sister, then Kathleen, to their chairs. The tables were set beautifully with fresh flower arrangements and the ship's best china and crystal. Kathleen shuddered to think of her last voyage in the bowels of steerage class. Arthur noticed her shiver but said nothing. The dinner passed pleasantly although Vivian said little, commenting only on the various dishes and listening attentively as the captain discussed the natives who would be greeting them at the next stop two days hence.

Arthur pressed Kathleen to describe her costume-designing experience and her plans for the Dublin Opera. The older man was quite aware of Kathleen's lie and knew there were a hundred ways he could catch her out, but instead he gently teased out her story, realizing he was listening to a young woman's dreams unfold. "I'm sure you're going to be just what Dublin needs," he said enthusiastically. "I suppose they'll be waiting at the gangplank with a band," he laughed.

Finally, awaiting their coffee and dessert, Kathleen inquired, "And you, where have you been traveling?" She nearly choked on Vivian's reply.

"Actually, Miss Evans, we've just come from Virginia City, a horrible place, simply horrible, but Arthur had to see for himself if their opera house was going to be finished in time." She preened for a moment, "You see, Arthur represents Italy's most famous opera star who is to perform there in early fall."

Arthur saw Kathleen's distress and admired her pluck but couldn't help asking, "Perhaps you know it?"

9.

The Opera House would be finished on time, partly thanks to Jack. Jack knew the mine owners and bankers were proud of having an opera house and the talent it had attracted, but it was clear that their money would be poured into the basic needs of the town, namely rebuilding the mining infrastructures, tunnels, trellises, stamping mills, and the like. And every man who could work on those projects would. So Jack took it upon himself to address his fellow lawmakers the next time the legislature met in Carson City. "What's them taxes for if they ain't to help promote the state?" he asked them. "Singing in Eye-talian and all that dancing around in feathers ain't my cup of tea, but there's plenty of other folks look at it as saving Virginia City from just being another rough old mining camp." He let the grumbling persist for a few minutes, just as he expected it would. "I say we stake the Piper family to a loan instead of expecting them to do the whole thing themselves," and here the grumbling increased ten-fold. "They give us a plan as to how long it's going to take and what's needed to get the doors open in time for that big opera star who's promised to play there, and we back 'em on it, fair and square."

Years of bartending had taught Jack a lot about human nature and that politics was basically horse-trading in suit coats, so naturally he had laid a bit of ground work. The senator from Carson City rose to address the body. "I think our colleague from Virginia City is a bit biased," he chortled, "but the man's right. When I travel to San Francisco, many of the businessmen I meet inquire about the opera house and when they might visit to see another production." He paused, "And I do believe they travel with their wallets open."

"Well, why don't we underwrite the whorehouses, too?" the representative from Tonopah asked. "They provide plenty of entertainment!"

"Yeah, and they take plenty out of your wallet, too!" yelled another gentleman as the house erupted in good-natured laughter.

Jack listened to the bantering and knew he had basically won the issue. Another confidante of his rose to make the motion. "I move we do just as the gentleman from Virginia City suggests, just as soon as a plan is brought before us and the finance committee can work out the details of the loan." Jack's other good friend, a former blackjack dealer from Reno, chaired the finance committee. The motion carried with only a few naysayers from the southern part of the State. Of course, Jack already had the Piper's plan and would leave it with the finance committee chair before he left town later in the day.

He left the capitol building in a buoyant mood but it was to be short-lasting as he saw the formidable widow Drake approaching him with her perpetually stern look. "Now here Jack Bartley, you wait up just a minute," she commanded him, red in the face from her exertion in trying to waylay him as he left the building. "You know I've left you a number of notes about a most urgent matter, and here I have to accost you on the street. Honestly," she puffed, "it's demeaning for a woman of my stature in the community."

Her stature was mostly stout, Jack thought to himself, but nonetheless doffed his hat. "Ah, Mrs. Drake, to what do I owe the pleasure on a spring day such as this?"

"I'm not going to stand on a street corner to discuss business with you like a common strumpet," she declared, linking her arm through his. "You'll walk me to my home and we'll have tea."

"Well, ma'am," Jack started, but his protest fell on deaf ears.

"Yes, I know you'd much rather be going to the Nugget for whiskey, but that is not happening this afternoon," and she tugged on his arm a bit harder. "Now, step lively. We have a lot to talk about."

Jack let himself be dragged down the street, amused at the looks they received from half the people they passed on the main street. They knew the widow Drake could be a force of nature, not a woman to be trifled with in the least, and whatever she wanted with Senator Bartley she would likely get before the afternoon was out.

10.

The widow Drake escorted Jack to the rooms she rented in the Swanson House, one of Carson City's original mansions on a slope just steep enough to provide a view of the capitol building and the surrounding Carson Valley. She bustled around taking off her cloak and hat while summoning a house maid to bring some tea and light refreshments which just happened to be neatly arranged on a silver serving tray. This had been no chance meeting, Jack realized, making himself as comfortable as possible on one of the dainty parlor chairs. As he crossed one leg over the other he couldn't help but notice Mrs. Drake's obvious distaste for the horse manure caked on the bottom of his boot and the dust on his pant legs. He quickly put both feet on the floor and kept them there.

Mrs. Drake barely waited for the weak tea to be served before she started in on her captive. "Now, Senator Bartley," she said sternly.

"Oh, call me Jack, ma'am," he interjected.

"I will do nothing of the sort, *Senator*." She paused before continuing in the same sharp tone. "I always stressed to Mr. Drake--may he rot in hell--that appearances are important and respect must be paid to those to whom it is due." Jack wasn't sure if that included him, but she forged on. "I believe as a Senator you have a certain responsibility to the citizenry of this State, as much as we do to you, sir." Jack felt certain that she muttered under breath, "and I use the term loosely," covering it with a cough.

"I'm just a plain-speaking man with some good old friends who saw fit to get me elected," Jack began. "Anyone calls me 'sir' I expect they're just wantin' somethin' from me." He looked the widow directly in the eye. "So what is it you're wantin?"

"I want nothing less than to make you the gentleman that I know you are capable of becoming," she stated firmly. "And to start that process, I want you to become my partner."

Jack nearly spit his tea in her face.

"Oh, you foolish man. You're all the same, thinking women want the same thing you do!" She blushed, nevertheless, thinking he might have entertained such a proposition for even an instant; perhaps she hadn't entirely lost her looks quite yet. "Now see here. I believe that what you've haven't drunk away or wasted on whores, you've probably put away." Jack looked appropriately chagrined but wasn't entirely surprised by the widow's well-known candor. "It just simply won't do for our senator to be living in a whore house some thirty miles from the capitol."

At this point, she stood up abruptly and motioned to Jack to follow her out of the parlor. "Now, I'm taking you upstairs, purely, and I do mean purely, to show you the rest of this lovely mansion. If you will follow me." Gathering her skirts she led Jack up the curving stairs to a broad landing off of which branched four bedrooms, each with their own sitting room. Jack dutifully stuck his head in each but still couldn't grasp the purpose of the tour. Ascending to the third floor, Jack saw a study with built-in bookshelves, a thick Persian carpet underneath a beautifully carved walnut desk. A bedroom flanked one side of the study and a small parlor the other. The entire third floor had windows all the way around, giving a view of the city from every room. The widow Drake pointed out details here and there, but Jack had stopped listening when he saw the third floor aerie. It was a space exactly befitting a bachelor Senator.

"I'll do it!" Jack said, running his hand over the desk. "I'll rent these here rooms from you."

"I never thought you would be one for such small thinking," the widow sighed. "Of course, you can't rent these rooms." Jack was visibly crestfallen. "You can't rent them from me because I don't own them. The home is still owned by the Swanson family, but they wish to sell and move to San Francisco. This is what I'm trying to tell you."

"Well, you've plain lost me," Jack shrugged.

"For heaven's sake man! I want you to be my partner in buying this lovely mansion and then *we* can rent out the rooms and have that income." The duo made their way back to the downstairs parlor, each deep in thought. "I propose to rent only to ladies, widows like myself," and she sternly eyed Jack. "You could have the third floor quarters, but there will be no monkey business with our tenants. These will be ladies, not the whores you're used to."

Jack still sat quietly which further exasperated his would-be partner. "Tell me that silver streak in your hair isn't reflective of a block of ore underneath it." Jack was vain about his looks, truth to tell, and had recently begun tying his long hair back in a ponytail in hopes of disguising the advancing gray. "I'll need an answer from you by the end of the week so that we can begin talking with the Swansons about the details." The widow Drake looked at Jack hopefully. "It would be nice to have a man in the house, after all."

"Well, ma'am," Jack said, stepping out onto the mansion's broad front porch, "it'll take some thinkin' but, a home might be just the thing…" He tipped his hat and stepped to the street. When he turned to look back up at the third floor turret, the widow Drake knew they had just forged a new relationship.

11.

Rounding the Horn was frightening indeed with gale force winds that threatened to blow the ship apart, but thankfully the most treacherous part of the journey was over within a few days and the ship entered much calmer waters with almost balmy temperatures in comparison. The passengers, Kathleen more so than most, took advantage of the opportunity to spend time on the deck, finding a trunk she could sit on that was sheltered by cargo and largely out of the wind. Here she took her sketch pad and designed a new gown nearly every afternoon. She could hardly wait to begin sewing her creations to see them come to life.

Kathleen was very surprised one afternoon to arrive at what she felt was 'her' place on the deck to find another passenger with a sketch book much like her own. "Well, hello! I see you've found the best place on board to work on your art," she told her fellow artist, a girl of about 12 with long blonde ringlets that seemed in sharp contrast to her serious demeanor.

"Yes, it is quite good to be out of the wind," the little girl replied, quickly closing her sketch book. "I'll leave you be."

"No, no," Kathleen said, squeezing in next to the girl. "Look, there's plenty of room for both of us. Please stay and show me your drawings." Seeing the girl's hesitation, Kathleen continued. "I'm Kathleen Evans, and I'd be pleased to show you my sketches, if you'd like to see them." The child was still reluctant, so Kathleen continued. "I'm sure your drawings are much better. I'm just doodling some silly dresses, is all."

At the mention of dresses, the girl's reserved manner thawed a bit. "I just draw people, you know, the sailors and the natives in the ports," she admitted. "My name is Viola," extending her hand to Kathleen and performing a slight curtsy.

"Viola! What a lovely name."

"My mother picked it. My father played the viola and she said he loved it so." Her smile was gone again and her shoulders slumped.

"Will your father be teaching you to play as well?" Kathleen asked innocently.

"No, he was killed. My mother, too." She turned her back to Kathleen who could see that she had begun to cry. She gently put her arm around Viola's shoulders and drew her back out of the wind to sit beside her. They stayed that way in silence for many minutes until finally Viola began her story. "They were coming home from the symphony. My mother had a blue silk gown on and my father was in his tuxedo, the one he wore to play with the orchestra. Their carriage was late so they decided to walk a ways." She sniffled. "A gang of robbers thought they were rich, I guess, and anyway..."

"Oh, honey, I'm so sorry." She held onto Viola until the girl stopped shaking. "Who are you with on the ship then?"

"My aunt and uncle, Arthur and Vivian. They thought it would be good for me to 'see the world', as they say." She actually laughed. "All I'm seeing is a lot of water, I think."

Kathleen had to laugh, too. "Yes, there is quite a lot of ocean in the world, isn't there?" She thought it best to add. "You know, I had dinner with your aunt and uncle a week or so ago. They seem very nice. I'm sure they love you very much, especially to take you on such a grand journey."

"They tell me they do, but they're old, you know," Viola said thoughtfully, "and I'm sure having a 12-year-old girl underfoot isn't what they expected."

"Life is hardly ever what we expect," Kathleen sighed. "Not even close."

12.

Philip was determined to play the new Steinway when Piper's Opera House officially reopened with the appearance of the famous Italian opera singer. He just had to get rid of his competition first. The Steinway was temporarily installed at the Millionaires' Club and every few days another pianist would step off the train, sheet music in hand, ready to audition. He had to admit that some of them were quite good, too. The better they played, the more foul Philip's mood became. On one such evening, he and Vicente sat at a table in the Corner Saloon, Vicente smoking vigorously and Philip pushing his drink around the table. "It's just not fair," he complained to Vicente. "I was their piano player before the fire and I should be guaranteed my position!"

"Oh, leave off with your whining," Vicente advised. "You know quite well what the problem is."

"No, why don't you remind me one more time," Philip snarled. "Just because the great opera star insists on practicing in the morning so he can sleep all afternoon, I have to give up my rightful position!" He slammed the glass on the table. "Why I have a mind to just bite them all, truly!"

Vicente grabbed Philip's hand in a vice grip. "You'll do nothing of the sort, and furthermore," he lowered his voice after first blowing out three concentric smoke rings, "you'll stop practically advertising your condition. What's the matter with you!" Vicente kept hold of Philip's wrist, watching his fledgling's frustration level edge higher and higher. "I know you feel like you've given up much of your freedom because of what I made you, but you've also gained much." Philip refused to look Vicente in the eye, but Vicente was not deterred. "Have you even practiced the piano one minute since Kathleen left? Have you?"

"I don't need to practice," Philip sulked. "I was good enough to play for the great Lotta Crabtree on her 'triumphant return' to the West, wasn't I?" Vicente had, in fact, seen the legendary star's performance at the Opera House before the fire and agreed that Philip's accompaniment was very good indeed. Actually, Vicente had become quite smitten with the petite entertainer, even following her performances in San Francisco. He didn't think he would ever get over Juliette, but still, he had always had an eye for the ladies.

"If you would sit down at the piano, I think you'd find that your skills have not diminished," Vicente said gently. "In fact, they have probably increased ten-fold." He let go of Philip's wrist. "I keep trying to tell you that there are certain compensations to our condition."

"Compensations my ass! I can't drink, can't eat, can't have sex, but now you're telling me I'll be able to play the piano ten times better, for a job I can't even get. That's just wonderful." Philip pushed his chair back angrily, then grabbed Vicente's wrist in turn. "Thank you so very much for everything you've done for me."

"Very well, go ahead and sulk, be as angry with me as you'd like." He easily slipped out of Philip's grasp. "I'm just saying, if I were you, I'd drop in at the Millionaires' Club some evening and play that Steinway." He clapped his hands together. "In fact, let's go tonight, the two of us."

But Philip was not to be talked out of his anger and frustration that easily. "I don't want to go anywhere with you. And you're not me, so don't think you know what I would do." He stormed out of the Corner Saloon, leaving Vicente to light another cigar.

"Ah, but I do know," Vicente mused to himself. Since he had made Philip a vampire, he was quite capable of reading — and if necessary — rearranging his thoughts. "Yes, I believe you will be dazzling the gents at the Millionaires' Club quite soon, quite soon."

13.

Jack never imagined owning a mansion or anything even close. He had been proud of the three-room house he'd built in Kentucky before the war. He and his wife often sat on the porch and talked about what additions they would add as more children came along. Jack thought he had put those days out of his memory but then some little thing would bring them rushing back, the sight of a child's toy in a yard, or two chairs side by side on a verandah. Of course, this house was a real estate deal, pure and simple, no sentiment about it. Actually, Jack liked talking about it that way and had already told Vicente and some of the other regulars at the Delta that he was "entering into a real estate deal" in the capitol city.

When Jack's banker friend, William Ralston, stopped in the Delta one night, Jack found himself eager to ask the banker's advice. "Say, Bill, let me get you a whiskey and let's talk for a minute." Ralston always liked Jack and was happy to have supported his bid for the state senate, but he was very surprised at Jack's news. "I'm thinking about entering into a real estate deal in Carson," Jack began. "You probably know the Swanson mansion up on Division Street." Ralston nodded that he did and encouraged Jack to go on. "Anyways, they're pulling up stakes and leaving for San Francisco so the place is for sale, and the widow Drake…"

Here Ralston stopped him. "Why that old battle axe!"

"Yeah, she's a crusty one all right, but she thinks we should buy the place and rent out rooms, just to proper ladies." He hastened to add, "And, I'd have the top floor to myself, three rooms and a view of the whole damn valley."

Ralston began to laugh. "Well, I do say that's a little like inviting the wolf into the hen house!"

"Nope, nothin' of the sort. The widow made it very clear," Jack replied, hoping the banker's raucous laughter wouldn't imply to the others that the deal was foolish. "Why, I like to think of myself as more of a lion in his lair, just watchin' out for the ladies."

"Well, you're the one who best be watching out," Ralston said seriously. "I think the widow would chop it off herself if she caught you fooling around." Then he continued. "You know the story about her husband, don't you?"

"I can't say as I've heard it, but he must have left her pretty well fixed," Jack acknowledged.

"He did that, my boy. She's got plenty of money. In fact, I don't know why she would want a partner in any deal." He began to laugh again. "She must see something special in you, by God."

"It's nothing like that," Jack stammered, although the widow's words about wanting to make him more of a gentleman did come back to him.

"Robert Drake was about the meekest man anyone had ever met," Ralston began. "If a par-boiled egg could walk and talk, that would have been him. But she was bound and determined to make him a pillar of industry, always pushing him into deals, or arrangements, as she liked to call them." One of the other Delta patrons spoke up, "He was a grocery clerk, but she wanted him to be wheeler-dealer, and he just didn't have it in him." Ralston nodded his agreement. "That woman just pushed and prodded him to no end, but finally I guess he'd had enough and off he went."

"Went where?" Jack asked. "I thought he was dead."

"Oh, he's dead all right. They found him a few weeks after he took off over the Sierras, bound for the city and ship back to England." Ralston paused in the story-telling. "I guess he decided he'd just as soon take his chances with the bears than spend another minute with that woman. Knowing old Drake, he probably just set down and politely let the bears make an evening meal of him."

The men gathered around the table laughed, but Jack found the tale unsettling. He'd have to watch the widow, he supposed, although no one had ever made him do anything he didn't want to, not even in the Army. He certainly wasn't about to let some 40-year-old woman put the spurs to him.

14.

Kathleen and Viola became like sisters in the weeks remaining in their sailing journey. They giggled like schoolgirls at some of the sailors' antics, their constant preening and posing to catch Kathleen's eye. If the seas were calm, as they often were now, the two would play hide-and-seek among the ship's cargo, but mostly they sat companionably side-by-side, drawing in their respective sketch books. Before Viola had become acquainted with Kathleen, she was largely a prisoner in her cabin, watched over by her aunt who worried that the sailors, or the natives in the various ports, might have kidnapped the precious little blonde, a rarity in that part of the world. Finally Arthur had to insist to his sister that Viola be allowed to spend time with Kathleen above decks.

"She's a no-nonsense young woman and it will be good for Viola to be exposed to someone like her," he emphatically told Vivian. "We must begin planning for our return home and seek an appropriate nanny or governess for the child, too."

Vivian started to protest that she herself was perfectly capable of taking care of their niece, but then thought better of it. "Yes, I expect I'll continue to be quite busy managing your schedule and the household in general," she demurred. "I don't think this Kathleen would be the person for the task, however. I think Viola should have a proper English woman, not some uneducated Irish seamstress."

Arthur wanted to come to Kathleen's defense but simply said, "Well, the girl's got a lot of pluck, I'll give her that." Any discussion of the necessary arrangements for Viola's upbringing was put off once again.

Meanwhile, Kathleen felt like she had assumed the role of Viola's teacher. The child had endless questions about all sorts of things, but quite often they came back to the same theme. Why would God let bad things happen to good people? Of course, Kathleen recognized Viola was recalling her parents' deaths. "If God loves us all the same, why do you think we're all different?" she asked one day. "Just look at that sailor, the fat one," she continued. "God wouldn't love him as much as he would the handsome one that's always trying to talk to you, would he?"

"Oh, I'm sure he would," Kathleen replied uneasily. She thought for a moment about how to make the youngster understand. "You know, I'm sure you have lots of dolls at home, don't you?" Viola agreed that she did, so Kathleen continued. "I'll bet you love all of them, don't you? And they're all different, am I right?"

"Well, sometimes I love one better than the other one," Viola stubbornly insisted. "And I'll bet God's that way, too."

Kathleen thought of Padraig and all the other miners who had perished in the fire. "You don't play with all the dolls at once, I'll bet, and maybe it's the same with God." She took Viola's hand. "God loves all of us, but he can't be *with* all of us all the time, maybe." She sighed. "Just think of all the people in the world."

After a moment, Viola responded. "You mean he couldn't be with Mommy and Daddy the night they were killed because maybe he had to be with someone else."

"Maybe, just maybe. And he knew you would still love him and that you'd be strong, that's what I think." Viola nodded but tears did escape each eye and she leaned in to Kathleen, accepting her embrace.

The whistle blew announcing the midday meal, so the two parted but not before making plans to meet again later in the afternoon and share their new drawings. Kathleen was still too embarrassed to take her meals in the main salon and chance running into Arthur and Vivian, so she retired to her cabin where she could also do more work on a little surprise she had planned for Viola when the ship reached London.

15.

With the loan from the legislature secured, work began around the clock on rebuilding the Opera House. Men worked day shifts in the mines replacing the burnt timbering, then reported at night to use their carpentering skills on building walls, replacing the ceiling on the three-story structure, and partitioning off the many rooms to be used for wardrobes, sets and suites for visiting performers. The masons worked one step behind them laying bricks and plastering the walls, and a small army of miscellaneous laborers carried out a myriad of chores, and so gradually the new Opera House began to take shape. An expert was brought in from New York City to oversee the positioning of the stage and the design of the orchestra pit, all to capture the appropriate acoustics.

Philip often came to the work site, usually just lingering in the wings, and was largely overlooked by the workers. He couldn't help but look to the area that used to house the wardrobe mistress. He half expected Kathleen to walk on stage with an armload of freshly ironed shirts or a new velvet jacket for the conductor. But he sensed she was still on her journey back to Ireland. He knew there would be no point in pursuing her; Vicente was correct about that, he had to admit. But still, if there were a chance to at least see her and know that she was safe…

On one such melancholy evening, Philip found himself drawn to the Millionaires' Club where the Steinway still resided, and where tonight Vicente had a front-row seat to another pianist's audition. Philip listened to the man pound away on the revered instrument until he could take it no longer. "Please, won't someone show this man the door!" he demanded. The pianist paused and lifted his hands from the keyboard, wherein Philip promptly slammed the lid shut on the keys and grabbed the man by the neck. Vicente leapt to restrain Philip but soon saw that all Philip intended was to wrest the man off the bench. That done, Philip promptly assumed the bench himself and gently slid the covering back from the ivories.

The candlelight reflecting off the gleaming ebony piano had the effect of making Philip appear almost ethereal, with his white skin, shining blue eyes and lustrous wavy blonde hair. It was quite intoxicating to Vicente, of course, but seemed to make the other men in the saloon uneasy in a way they couldn't have defined if asked. He played slowly at first, barely letting his fingers graze the keys, without a sheet of music in front of him. He played two or three songs that the more cultured men in the saloon would have been familiar with but then tossed back his blonde mane and leaned closer to the piano. His position was almost intimate but his facial expression was fathomless.

Very gradually Philip's tapered fingers sought keys further up and down the scale, first slowly, then faster. By now the patrons had put down their drinks and even Vicente snubbed out his cigar; they knew they were witnessing something extraordinary. The few women allowed in the exclusive saloon, basically the bar maids and a cigarette girl, felt they might swoon, and even some of the men had removed their handkerchiefs and were alternately patting their brows or fanning themselves. Although only one listener realized he was hearing Chopin's etudes, notably number three, Tristesse, everyone was moved nearly to tears, recognizing the sadness of the melody and the artistry of Philip's presentation. When Philip at last touched the final note, he rose and bowed deeply to the spellbound audience. Vicente fought back a smug expression when Philip glanced his way then hurried from the club.

The gentleman who was familiar with the etudes, and had, in fact, heard the 23-year-old Chopin play in the salons of Paris, was too overcome to approach Philip but instead penned a hastily written note which he pressed into Vicente's hand, recognizing him as a friend of the young virtuoso. "Young sir, please do me the honor of dining with me Saturday hence at nine in the evening, in my home. You know it as the former Mackay mansion. It will be my exquisite pleasure to discuss a fulfilling arrangement for all concerned at the Opera House when it reopens." And the note was signed, Charles Piper, the impresario who had been able to induce the greatest operatic tenor in the world to perform on opening night, a scant six weeks away.

16.

The widow Drake drove a hard bargain for the Swanson mansion, and at times in the negotiations Jack was alternately embarrassed and impressed at what she asked for—and what she got in the deal. "If you was horse tradin', you'd ask for a spare leg to be thrown in, I swear," he laughed when they left the bank offices. "I expect the Swansons feel like they've been dragged through a crushing machine."

"I suppose you'd rather have them laughing at us all the way to San Francisco," the widow said. In a more conspiratorial tone, she added, "A person hears things, and apparently the Swansons were in rather a hurry to get out of Carson City, and indeed, out of the state completely, certain of their business dealings not being entirely up to snuff it seems."

When they approached the stately mansion, their new home, Jack found himself truly moved. While the widow hurried up the steps, key in hand, Jack hung back admiring the broad wrap-around porch with its wide steps and the impressive oak front door. Shrubs lined the granite walkway up to the house and defined the front borders of the yard. In back, a row of cottonwood trees provided shaded areas. A bench would be nice out there, Jack thought, or some chairs where friends could gather. The ladies could plant some roses, too.

"Senator, where are you? Stop dawdling out there. We have things to do to get this house in shape," the widow called out. "Step lively, will you?"

Jack could feel his resolve to be the man of the house being chipped away already, but he smiled thinking of his own private quarters and how pleasing it would be to sit at that great desk in the tower with a whiskey in hand, smoking a cigar (if she let him!). The Swansons had indeed left in a hurry, Jack could see when he entered the foyer. The house was still largely furnished, although a few of the tables had been tipped on their sides. He set to straightening things up while the widow went through each room, talking to herself, he assumed, about what would be needed in each room. Jack expected to bring a change or two of clothes, a shaving brush and razor, and not much else since he felt he would still be expected to spend most of his time with his constituents in Virginia City. That, and the fact that he still enjoyed an occasional trip upstairs to the whores at the Delta, something he knew the widow would discourage.

"So the first thing you must do is go to the newspaper and place this advertisement," the widow said, thrusting a piece of paper at Jack. "It is the announcement that we," she hesitated, "or perhaps it should say 'I' am accepting applications from reputable ladies seeking private, long-term accommodations in the newly renovated Blake Mansion."

"Where's the Blake mansion?" Jack asked dumbly.

"Don't you see — it's a combination of our names, Drake and Bartley!" She sighed, "Honestly, I do wonder about how you were elected. Politicians are usually clever, at least."

"I told you I weren't no politician," Jack defended himself. "And that ain't much of a combination anyway. Everybody will still call it the Swanson place."

"We'll just to see to it that they *don't*," the widow stated emphatically. "When 'Blake Mansion' appears often enough in the society columns and the like, people will forget all about those carpet-bagging Swansons."

Jack was forced to concede and grabbed his hat for the stroll down to the Nevada Appeal offices. Along the way he met several men he knew, either from the saloons or from the legislature, so he decided to practice his new role. "Yep, just headin' to the paper to put an advertisement in for my new business venture," he told one such encounter. "Me and the widow Drake are opening the Blake Mansion for women here shortly." Meeting another man, he phrased it slightly differently. "The proper single ladies in this town need a nice safe place to live, so the widow Drake and I have invested in a mansion." Then pushing his chest out, "We'll be shortly turning the Blake Mansion into just such an address." But no matter how he phrased it, the questions were always the same. "Where's the Blake mansion?" And just as often, "How the hell'd you get tied up with that battleaxe?"

He felt rather dispirited by the time he reached the newspaper where the editor gave him a further grilling on his new venture. He paid for the ad space but doubted it would even be necessary. Word of mouth in the small town would beat the morning newspaper.

17.

One crystal-blue morning Viola and Kathleen sat on deck, each bent over their sketch books, when suddenly Viola jumped up excitedly and pointed off to the distance. "Is that a whale? Is it?" she shrieked with delight. Kathleen immediately ran to the railing to see for herself, but seeing nothing she turned back to Viola, only to see that little scamp running down the deck with Kathleen's sketch book in hand!

"You bring that back here right now!" Kathleen yelled at the girl, following her down the deck under the bemused eyes of the sailors. Viola had quickly climbed to the top of one of the piles of cargo, however, holding the sketch book aloft.

"No! You can only have it back if you come to dinner with auntie and uncle tonight," Viola proclaimed. She knew Kathleen had assiduously avoided every such invitation.

"Oh, you little…witch! You just wait," Kathleen threatened her. That sketch book meant more to her than any possession she had. "All right then, dinner it is, but you can be sure I'm going to tell on you, let them know just what a mean little girl you are!" She laughed despite trying to appear stern. "And I'm going to be sure they make you eat whatever scaly, slimy fish they put on your plate, little girl!" Before she completely broke down in laughter, Kathleen turned on her heel and determinedly made her way down the deck and back to her cabin.

Viola waited until she was sure Kathleen was in no position to ambush her, then quickly stole back to her own cabin. She was eager to make her own additions to Kathleen's sketches and spent the rest of the afternoon doing so. Kathleen meanwhile was sewing in her cabin and practicing what she might say to Arthur and Vivian during that evening's dinner.

Arthur had witnessed the little interchange between the two girls from the vantage point of the captain's cabin and wondered what had transpired to separate them so early in the afternoon. He was surprised to find Viola back in the cabin, bent over a sketch book, something she normally would have been doing above-decks with Kathleen. "So, what are we drawing today, dear?" he asked as he bent over to catch a glimpse, but Viola anticipated the move and quickly covered the book.

"It's a surprise. You'll see at dinner when Kathleen comes."

"She's joining us for dinner, is she? Your invitation must have been quite persuasive." He patted the precocious child on her shoulder and went off to announce the news to Vivian whom he suspected might be less than thrilled.

Kathleen put the finishing touches on her parting gift for Viola then dressed carefully for dinner, anxious not to appear the Irish country girl that she was in reality. When the ship's bells announced the call to the evening meal, she nearly backed out, but she had to retrieve her sketches. As she entered the salon, Arthur and Vivian were already there, Viola seated between them and looking ready to burst with excitement. "See! She's here. I knew she would be," the little girl squirmed with delight.

After exchanging greetings with Viola's aunt and uncle, Kathleen looked sternly at Viola. "And do you have my sketch book?"

"Oh, that. Hmmm. I thought maybe I'd make you wait until after dessert," Viola giggled, but she slid the book out from behind her on the settee. Kathleen wanted to pounce on it, but Viola held it firmly. "I want to show you what I did first." With that she opened page after page of Kathleen's dress and costume sketches, but Viola had added something important to each. "See here? That's Enrico Caruso, the opera singer." She pointed to another of Kathleen's designs where she had added another face and delicate arms. "That's Maria," she hesitated and turned to Arthur, "Uncle, what's Maria's last name, you know, the one who came to tea that day?" Arthur supplied the name and Viola went on with her presentation of Kathleen's sketches.

Kathleen was astonished but Arthur was more so. Viola's addition of faces and figures to the costumes brought them to life. Kathleen saw how beautifully Viola could draw people, but Arthur saw Kathleen's exquisite eye for both design and functionality in the costumes. Opera singers and most theater performers were robust, full-figured presences, and Kathleen had designed with them in mind instead of drawing outfits only a street urchin could wear. "They're extraordinary, truly extraordinary!" Arthur exclaimed, Vivian nodding in agreement.

"Oh, yes, Viola has quite a talent," Kathleen agreed, still stunned at what she was seeing."

"Oh, not at all, I mean, yes, quite," Arthur stammered. "What I mean is that you, young woman, have quite a talent of your own. These designs are just stunning!"

Kathleen blushed but could say nothing. She herself was overwhelmed. But Viola had one more surprise for Kathleen before she surrendered the sketch book. On the last page was a drawing she had done of Kathleen sitting in repose, gazing out at the ocean, the ship's sails unfurled in the background. She captured Kathleen's presence and bearing exactly. But standing off to the side of Kathleen and slightly behind her was another figure, a man with flowing blonde hair unlike any of the sailors on the ship. "Why, who is that?" Kathleen asked uneasily.

"It's the man who watches over you," Viola replied. The captain's steward then called them in to dinner.

18.

When the evening came for Philip to present himself to Charles Piper's mansion, Vicente appeared at the mouth of the tunnel they more or less shared, elaborately attired in a navy blue velvet smoking jacket, black silk blend slacks, a blue-gray silk shirt with onyx buttons and cuff links, and black suede boots. He carried a walking stick with an elaborately carved goat head on top and draped a cape over his arm. Philip was in a plain black wool suit with gray calf-skin gloves and looked at Vicente uncomprehendingly. "And for what soiree are you so elaborately attired?" he inquired of the elder vampire.

"Why yours, of course!" He could see that Philip was immediately resistant but didn't allow him to voice the first objection. "You're not going to haggle with Jack at the Delta about playing a few songs in the saloon a couple nights a week." He puffed his chest out. "You need an experienced negotiator," and here he drew himself up to his full height, "me."

"I know fully well what Mr. Piper wants," Philip countered. "And I know what I want. No daytime practice sessions and my name directly below the conductor's in the program." He was betting Vicente hadn't thought of that.

"Oh, pshaw, foolish boy," Vicente said. "Those are trifles. Mr. Piper is going to want you to sign your life away — to him. He'll probably offer you a handsome sum for the night of the opera but then insist you play in any show he produces, for a pittance." He sighed. "These show people. I've been around them since you were a boy, since well before you were a boy, since well before your father was…"

"Yes, I get it," Philip interjected impatiently. "You were around when dirt was invented." He poked Vicente in the chest, "I, Philip Evans, was invited to dinner—alone! It would be rude to show up with some other uninvited guest."

"No matter, my boy, I already sent word along yesterday that as your manager, of course I would be accompanying you," Vicente said smugly, brushing aside Philip's finger. "Mr. Piper's assistant assured me I would be most welcome indeed." He brushed a bit of dust off Philip's drab jacket. "So, shall we?" Philip recognized there was no point in arguing, and the pair made their way down the hill to where Vicente's elegant carriage stood waiting.

A white gingerbread porch surrounded the brick mansion on all four sides with a brick pathway leading to the front door, flanked by floor-to-ceiling windows. While the top floor remained dark, the bottom had welcoming lights in each window. Mr. Piper himself answered the door as soon as he heard the carriage arrive. "Welcome, welcome," he heartily greeted the men as they alighted, nearly thrown off balance by the always skittish horses. He put his arm lightly around Vicente's shoulders and motioned for Philip to follow them into the parlor where a butler awaited.

Piper moved to shake Philip's hand which the pianist did, but only for an instant and without removing his gloves. "Well," Piper said, looking a bit miffed. "I believe it's customary for a gentleman to remove his gloves before shaking hands with another."

"Oh, I expect you're right. It just shows my poor upbringing on a farm and all," Philip replied ingratiatingly, "plus, you know, I watch out for my hands." He did not want to undergo the shocked reaction his host would have had at touching his stone-cold fingers on a relatively balmy evening. Vicente avoided the same situation by busying himself with his cape and cane, handing both to the butler, then clasping his hands behind his back and leaning away from the other gentlemen to examine a map of the Comstock on the parlor wall.

Vicente had already schooled Philip on how to avoid the awkwardness of neither drinking nor eating, with sleight-of-hand movements that would easily fool Piper or any serving staff present. Indeed, the dinner and postprandial brandies passed quite smoothly with the men discussing the progress on the Opera House and the rebuilding of the town in general. Finally, it was time for the business at hand. Piper began. "Your performance at the Millionaires' Club was enough for me to cancel any further auditions, son." Clearing his throat, "I believe you're the only one for the job, and I've already wired our star to tell him we have the pianist of his dreams awaiting."

"Hmm, well, that's very flattering, and of course, very true," Vicente began. "But there are a myriad of considerations to Philip's employment."

Piper was annoyed at the interruption, believing the farm boy, as he described himself, would simply have jumped at the chance to perform with the great opera singer. But, he had spent time in Europe and had seen men such as this (or so he suspected). "Yes, and I'm so happy you're here to discuss those on his behalf." He offered Vicente a cigar which the 'manager' eagerly accepted; the butler was on hand to light it expertly, a gesture Vicente appreciated. "I've taken the liberty of drawing up a contract for your—and Philip's—review," Piper said, extending a single-page document to Vicente.

"As you said earlier, we still have a few weeks until opening night, so that gives us ample time to review your offer," Vicente said, motioning Philip to nod in agreement. "I believe we'll take this with us and get back to you in the days to come, won't we Philip?" Philip nodded again although he was seething at Vicente's interference. Vicente stood to leave and took Philip by the elbow.

"It won't be long, sir," Philip volunteered. "I certainly appreciate the opportunity and I can tell you that no performance will be the equal of mine—now or at any time in the future."

"Quite so, my boy, quite so," Piper said, still endeavoring unsuccessfully to shake Philip's hand. The butler showed the men to their carriage. As the stallions thundered off down the canyon he too felt a certain unease with the men and he hoped his employer knew what lay ahead.

19.

Jack had taken to dressing better, or cleaner at least, cussin' less and hardly using ain't no more, not that it was easy. This was all under the direction of the widow Drake, of course, whose influence he could not escape whether he was in his third-floor rooms at the mansion or jawin' with the Vicente and the whores at the Delta. If he decided to let loose on a Saturday night, it was always in the back of his mind that he had to be at the Blake Mansion for Sunday dinner, something Mrs. Drake insisted on having promptly at two in the afternoon; it left very little time to sweat out the Saturday night whiskey and catch the train down into Carson City. If he were forced to admit it, however, those Sunday dinners were the best time of the week.

"It's just dizzyin' the way their minds work," Jack expounded to Vicente one evening. "Those little gals can spend an hour dissecting two sentences some man said to them, they come to agreement, you'd think, then boom, the whole thing changes direction." He chuckled, "They remind me of the dust devils the mustangs kick up in the desert." He regarded Vicente. "I'd invite you to dinner some Sunday but I know you keep your days to yourself…you and Philip, I guess."

"That's very kind of you to think of me, Jack, but I think hearing you tell the stories about these ladies is almost as fun as being there," Vicente said gallantly. "And you're right, our days are taken up with Philip's preparation for the Opera House performance and my own financial management details." He added, "It keeps us both quite busy."

"The widow is busy, too. We finally got us a full house and she's the mother hen, even though two of the boarders are older than she is, I'd say." He went on to describe the women in all eight rooms in the mansion. "I'd say it'd be easier to pass muster in the army than it would be to live under her roof full-time." The women boarders all had to pass an interview before being granted an invitation to live in the mansion, though Jack steered clear of that process. "She's got a rule for everything. The ladies can't even come out of their rooms in their housecoats. She says they have to be fully dressed, even if they're just flittin' down to the kitchen for a cup of coffee. And," Jack added with emphasis, "Get this. Before they go out anywhere in town, they have to pass the widow's inspection, hat, gloves, the whole shootin' match. She says in that screechy voice of hers, 'I won't have anyone thinking we have anything but first-class accommodations and first-class guests in them,' and they go along with it—or they get the boot."

"And I suppose she inspects you as well?" Vicente couldn't resist teasing his old friend. "Suit pressed, shirt starched, boots shined, nails clean?"

"Oh, I'd like to see her try!" Jack was now happy Vicente wasn't going to one of the Sunday dinners because that was exactly the scrutiny he underwent before being admitted to his seat at the head of the table. The widow had hired an excellent cook, Jack had to admit, and the Sunday dinners were full of spirited discussion, often about men and their shortcomings, Jack acknowledged, although the women were very respectful of him. He suspected the widow had warned them off; she certainly told him they were strictly off-limits. "These women were wives, Senator Bartley. I'm sure you recall your wife and how you would like her treated." He had never told her the story about his wife and, indeed, how poorly she was treated in his absence. But, his wedding ring must have told the tale. Sometimes when Jack climbed the stairs to his rooms he could hear the other women, talking quietly with each other, laughing, and often as not, crying alone in their rooms. There was a lot of sorrow and hard times in the world, he reflected, and it seemed that women got more than their share.

20.

Arthur had come to enjoy his breakfasts with the ship's captain. He liked to pore over the navigational charts and learn just how many more days their journey would last. Of course, the captain had many ribald tales about ports around the world and the women who awaited him there. But ever since seeing Kathleen's sketch book, Arthur cut the tale-telling time short, confirmed the ship's likely arrival date and hastened back to his room where he furiously wrote letters for the remainder of the day, not to be disturbed even for the midday meal.

Kathleen and Viola became nearly inseparable as the days ticked off until the ship would sail into the London harbor. They continued their sketching and Viola often delighted one of the sailors or a fellow passenger with a sketch of themselves. Her talent was blossoming along with her personality and it was often hard for Kathleen to believe Viola was only a 12-year-old girl. Nothing intimidated her, it seemed, but Kathleen worried that the girl's open, trusting manner would be a problem for her in the future; she hoped the McDougalls had made plans for her education, although she would never venture to discuss the matter with them. She had at last gotten over her embarrassment at sharing their dinner table, and even frosty Vivian had warmed up to Kathleen and asked her opinion about her own dresses. Kathleen was careful not to tell her the truth, however, and she saw the twinkle in Arthur's eyes whenever she delivered a diplomatic assessment.

On the last night before approaching London, the final stop for most of the passengers, the Captain's Dinner would be held, a gala for which everyone was expected to dress their best. Kathleen had remade one of her rather plain traveling suits by cinching in the waist, broadening the lapels, and cutting a daring slit up the side of the skirt. She added jeweled buttons she had stitched by hand from the semi-precious stones that she had bought by the cupful in one of the South American ports. A pert little hat was made all the more interesting by the addition of a colorful peacock feather, the lighter green of the feather contrasting with the deep emerald of the suit. She wore her red hair loose over her shoulders. Just the stroll from her cabin to the main salon confirmed that she had achieved a dramatic effect as sailors bowed deeply and entreated her in a half-dozen languages to marry them! She simply smiled but nevertheless felt glamorous and alluring.

Earlier that afternoon she had presented Viola with her parting gift, an exquisitely made velvet evening purse in the deep purple Viola preferred, accented with a woven golden drawstring and a clasp with lavender and silver sequins. Inside Kathleen had sewn an inscription. "Made only for Viola McDougall by her forever friend Kathleen Evans." It was a small conceit, Kathleen realized, to put her own name on the creation, but she had already decided to do so with every gown or costume she would make in the years to come. Lying in bed in the early mornings, she already envisioned actresses and socialites arriving at the shop of Kathleen Evans, begging for their own special, one-of-a-kind gown. In her daydreams, she would sometimes acquiesce to make such a gown, but at other times she would put the demanding woman off until she nearly begged. She would chide herself then. "That would be the day when you would be in the position to turn away work!" Still, the harmless fantasies kept her focused on the future rather than dwelling in the past.

Kathleen sternly made Viola promise not to cry when she saw her gift, nor when she left the ship the next morning, leaving Kathleen behind to sail on to Dublin. Viola struggled with the promise as did Kathleen, and finally both broke down, but Kathleen said, "Now we must stop this so our eyes don't puff up like old bags," and she mooed like a cow. The silly gesture worked and the two were able to part laughing before they went off to dress for dinner, Viola swinging her purse over her shoulder, then clutching it to her chest.

When Kathleen entered the salon, every eye turned her way, an experience quite new to her but entirely thrilling. When she approached the McDougall's table, Arthur immediately jumped to his feet, Kathleen assumed to surrender his chair to her, but instead the elderly man took her by the elbow. "Can we step into the captain's cabin for a moment?" She hesitated, thinking it was some last-minute ploy, but he added, "We must talk about the future." She received a nod from Vivian and a little shooing motion from Viola, so Kathleen took his arm and the two went upstairs to the captain's private quarters.

"I assume you want to talk about Viola's future," Kathleen began as soon as they were seated.

"Oh, no, not at all—I mean not that I'm *not* concerned, but it's *your* future that occupies me tonight," he said solemnly, withdrawing a folder of papers from inside his coat jacket. "Let us drop our little charade, shall we, on this final night together?"

Kathleen blushed but held her head up high. "I'm sure I don't know what charade you refer to, sir."

Arthur sighed and tried to relax. "Young lady, I'm well acquainted with the Dublin Opera and know that they could not possibly have already hired you to be their designer, wardrobe mistress, or even a lowly seamstress." He saw Kathleen start to tear up. "But I predict that they will—and soon—and many other companies will be standing in line to receive even a moment of your attention." He untied the ribbon around the sheaf of papers. "I have written letters of recommendation on your behalf to every theater company, every opera house, every stage manager I know in Ireland and England; you need only present a letter to a group you feel worthy of your immense talent."

Kathleen was stunned at this huge gesture and accepted the packet with trembling hands. "I don't…"

Arthur clasped her hands. "Don't say anything. A few months from now when I see your designs step on stage, that will be thanks enough, to know that I could help bring such beauty into the world." He took a second smaller packet out of his jacket. "This is a list of reputable homes where I believe you could find suitable rooms, again with my recommendation." When Kathleen unfolded the papers, several hundred pound notes were ensconced within, but Arthur simply tucked them back in with the other papers and retied the silk string around them. "Now, let's not keep the captain waiting!" He helped Kathleen to her feet and put his hand at the small of her back to guide her down to the salon and an evening that certainly had no match in Kathleen's life to this point.

21.

The big night had finally arrived. The Opera House was filled
to overflowing with Virginia City's elite and even a few
visitors from San Francisco. Charles Piper had even arranged
for a small standing-room-only section at the back of the
house and that too was packed. The red velvet stage curtain
hung in perfectly pleated folds; it exactly matched the fabric
on the seats. For aesthetic and acoustic purposes, a moiré silk
covered the walls, and richly woven carpets marked the aisles.
The orchestra could be heard making a few last-minute
adjustments. Women in ball gowns fanned themselves with
their programs; even these had been printed with gilt edges
for the special occasion. At last the gas lamps were dimmed
and the crowd murmured a sigh of excitement as the
conductor strode to center stage. Should they applaud now or
later? Their excitement overcame them and they clapped
loudly until the conductor signaled them to stop. They barely
heard his announcement about the evening's program as their
anticipation grew to see the famous Italian tenor take the
stage.

Earlier in the day newspaper reporters from throughout the
state as well as from New York City and San Francisco
crowded the railroad platform hoping to catch a quote from
the great star as he disembarked from the train. His manager
disappointed them all by explaining that the tenor had to
adjust to the great altitude and dryness of the desert and
therefore had to preserve his voice for that night's
performance. Nevertheless, the reporters wrote about the
huge number of wardrobe trunks and accoutrements traveling
with the star, and they described him in great detail as well,

although a lot of the townsfolk were already there at the depot to enjoy the spectacle for themselves.

Jack and the banking and railroad barons arrived before the performance, meeting in The Corner Saloon adjacent to the Opera House to enjoy a whiskey or two; those who were married had already arranged for carriages to collect their wives in enough time to allow them a grand arrival in gowns ordered especially for the occasion. "Honestly, Jack, I wondered if we'd ever see the day," Ralston began and the others nodded in agreement. "That loan scheme of yours was just the ticket." He slapped Jack on the back. "Now, if you'd just do something about the mines petering out." The knot of men laughed, but cautiously, as concern about the dwindling silver output had everyone concerned.

When the tenor stepped on stage, however, these concerns were put aside. Jack felt proud to see Philip seated at the magnificent Steinway, and as he began to play and the tenor to sing, he felt choked up inside with pride and a dozen other emotions. Even the most sophisticated residents who claimed to have heard opera in the great cities of Europe were stunned at the power and clarity of the performance. The tenor was a man in his forties with a great barrel chest and jet-black hair, slicked straight back from his broad forehead. His slacks appeared to be black satin and his jacket was a burgundy velvet with black satin lapels, overtop a black shirt open several buttons. Curiously, when he reached the most tender portion of the aria, he chanced to look to the front row and seemed instantly mesmerized. Many in the audience noticed it and craned their necks to see the object of his fascination. Even Jack leaned over the railing in his box to see and was greatly amused that the tenor had set his sights on the widow Drake, for whom Jack had obtained a ticket some months earlier. Well, he knew he would be hearing about this night at Sunday dinners for months to come.

The ovations went on and on at the end of the spectacular performance, with the tenor taking bow after bow. Philip and the conductor enjoyed repeated curtain calls as well. Finally, Piper ordered the gas lights to be raised and walked onto the stage himself to tumultuous applause. He quieted the vast hall, then said, "We have one man in particular to thank for this night's performance," and with that he pointed up to the box where Jack sat. Vicente saw Jack was half-asleep and poked him awake. Piper continued, "Senator Jack Bartley stepped up to help rebuild this hall and indeed, to rebuild Virginia City. This is an example of what government can do when it works *for* the people." Several of the men in the audience shouted, "Hear, hear," and the ladies looked admiringly toward Jack. The newspapermen scribbled furiously and several rushed upstairs hoping to get a quote from the senator himself. Jack flashed his usual self-deprecating smile and waved at the audience. Vicente whispered in his ear, "This virtually assures you'll be the next governor of Nevada, you know."

22.

There was a throng of private carriages, draught wagons and every other form of cargo conveyance gathered at the wharf when the ship arrived in the London harbor. Vivian insisted Viola hold her hand at all times in the confusion, but Viola had to break away for one last hug from Kathleen. They each had promised not to cry but found it impossible not to. Most of the passengers were disembarking in London and Viola pleaded with Kathleen to do the same. "You can come live with us. I know uncle would allow it," she cried. "He could help you get work and you could help me, and…" The little girl was overcome, but Kathleen tried to reassure her.

"Your uncle has been most generous with his help already," she tried to explain, "and you're so smart and so talented you don't need my help."

"Oh, but I do," Viola sobbed. "I don't have anyone watching over me like you do!"

This gave Kathleen the shivers, but she put her arm around the girl's shoulders and walked her back to her waiting aunt and uncle. "You'll have such a grand life, I just know it." She hesitated just a little, "And you do have people watching over you, and I will, too." Viola was inconsolable but it was time for them to leave the ship. Vivian hugged Kathleen briefly and Arthur took her hands in his.

"Now you must write to us and let us know how you're getting on," he encouraged her. "I know things will work out splendidly for you. Little Viola needs to know that the world will welcome a talented woman like yourself, and like her, so I hope you two will correspond and perhaps you'll even come to visit us."

"You've been too kind," Kathleen began, but Arthur stopped her from thanking him any further. Vivian called that their carriage was waiting and admonished Arthur to double-check that they had all of their baggage. As he turned to leave, he said quickly, "Please, just make me proud."

The continuation of the trip to Dublin was mercifully short and Kathleen spent all of it in her cabin. She was terribly sad to be leaving Viola and the security of the McDougalls but at the same time found herself unable to sleep at night for the plans and dreams spinning in her mind. She looked forward to being immersed in Irish culture again and hearing Gaelic spoken on the streets. The letters of introduction from Arthur would open so many doors, she was certain, hopefully the first door being one where she might live.

When her ship entered the Dublin harbor Kathleen was among the first passengers to leave the ship. She hadn't expected any fanfare for the returning Irish and the handful of English passengers and therefore wasn't disappointed. With the money Arthur had given her she was able to charter a private carriage and gave the driver the address of one of the rooming houses Arthur had recommended. When the carriage came to a halt she was surprised to see a veritable mansion instead of the tenements the Irish had gotten so used to in New York. The woman who answered Kathleen's knock at the door was dressed simply, not like a maid but not like the owner of such a grand home either.

Kathleen began her introduction in Gaelic but soon saw the woman didn't understand so switched to English. "I've been advised that perhaps you have rooms to let?" She prepared to feel foolish, thinking perhaps Arthur got the address wrong, but the woman smiled broadly and gestured Kathleen into the parlor.

"Now who would have advised you of such a thing, dear?" the lady asked, still smiling.

"I have here a letter from Arthur McDougall, introducing myself," Kathleen stammered.

"Oh Arthur! How wonderful! Is he well? Is he in Dublin then? And how do you know him?" The rapid-fire questions surprised Kathleen but at least she knew she had the correct address.

"We have just completed a journey, on ship, from San Francisco, and he…"

The woman's raised eyebrows revealed Kathleen's mistake. "I should say, I made Mr. McDougall's acquaintance on the ship courtesy of his lovely niece, Viola, and his sister, Vivian. Perhaps you know them as well?"

"I did meet Vivian once, which was quite enough," the woman said chuckling. "Now, come into the parlor and let's have some tea. You can tell me exactly what brings you here." She rang a small bell for a maid and requested she bring some tea and some sandwiches. Kathleen tried to politely refuse, but she was famished and when the food came quickly ate several of the delicate little treats as well as a piece of chocolate candy.

"I am returning to Ireland to design costumes for the theater," Kathleen began, a little self-consciously, "so I need a place to live and perhaps a small studio for my work, but I can't imagine a house this grand would actually…"

"Nonsense. A house 'this grand' as you put it, costs money to run and since my husband died, if I want to stay here I have to finance it. So, yes, I am taking boarders." Kathleen looked relieved but the woman had more to say. "I'll have no carrying on with men here, understand that, and I'll expect you to help with things from time to time."

"Oh, I have no intention of carrying on with anyone, and yes I'd be happy to help with anything," Kathleen said eagerly. "I should say, name is Kathleen Evans, as you'll see on Mr. McDougall's letter, originally from County Cork. I have no family and my work will be my life, a most quiet one, you'll see."

"Oh, a young lady like you with that beautiful red hair can't be hoping for *that* quiet a life, I hope," her new landlady laughed. "I myself am Beatrice Wellington, although you may call me Bea." With that, she extended her hand to Kathleen, "Welcome to Castle Wellington, be it ever so humble." Kathleen had already warmed to her easy manner and felt it was a positive sign of things to come.

23.

After the tenor's performance, the usual group of men returned to The Corner Saloon, this time joined by Philip and Vicente. Everyone who walked through the saloon doors came to shake Jack's hand or slap him on the back in congratulations. They extended a new level of respect to Philip too, teasing him that his playing had certainly improved since his days of pounding on the old upright piano in the Delta.

"The only distracting part of your performance tonight was your constant looking off-stage," Vicente began to lecture Philip. "But otherwise…"

"I kept thinking she would walk out of wardrobe and bring me a fresh shirt or straighten my sheet music."

Of course, Vicente knew who Philip so wistfully referred to. "Well, she's not going to, not tomorrow night, not ever," he said, not meaning to be cruel.

"I just wish, well I just wish I knew how she was," Philip admitted, twisting the wedding band he still wore.

"You didn't believe me when I talked to you about the compensations of our condition, but look how well you play now, a level you never could have attained…before." Vicente added, "So believe me now when I tell you that you can check in on Kathleen any time you wish. If you had a strong connection to her…"

"I did. You know I did. I loved her, still love her," the young man stated.

"Well then, use that connection to just visualize her," Vicente instructed him. "You'll see her exactly although she won't necessarily be aware of you."

Philip stared at Vicente, then closed his eyes, interlocked his fingers beneath his chin and appeared to concentrate totally. In moments a smile spread across his face. "Yes, I do see her." He appeared lost in the moment but then told Vicente. "She is in Dublin in a lovely set of rooms, she is sewing and seems completely content." He paused, "It should make me sad, but it doesn't."

Jack stopped by their table at just this moment, too wound up to sit at his own table and accept all the accolades coming his way. "So what do you gents have your heads together about?" He lit a cigar for Vicente, then complimented Philip on his performance. "Too bad Kathleen wasn't here to hear that, all right, but I expect she knows you're a star tonight," he said, hoping to cheer Philip out of a certain dark mood he'd been in for months. "The newspaper boys will be writing up everything and I imagine she'll read about it, wherever she is." Jack could tell his comments weren't really helping though, so he decided to move on.

He was in high spirits and normally in a mood like this he would have spent the night with one of the whores from the Delta or one of other brothels, but now he began to truly feel like the next governor of Nevada, and he could hear the widow Drake's words in the back of his head. "Appearances, Senator, appearances matter." He supposed he would just catch the last train down to his rooms in Carson City after all. The last he had seen the widow she was headed backstage at the opera house, carrying a huge bouquet of roses that the tenor had passed to her from the stage. Somehow though Jack didn't believe she'd be spending the night in Virginia City either.

24.

Just as Arthur's letter of introduction had opened the door to a wonderful rooming situation for Kathleen, his letters to the theater personnel had a similar effect. Kathleen realized that she could study the playbills advertising upcoming performances to see who would be in the cast, then sketch a costume that exactly captured the performer and the role; all she lacked was Viola's ability to draw in the face. When she presented these sketches to the theater managers or show directors, along with Arthur's letter, her reception was overwhelmingly positive.

Within a matter of months Bea had suggested Kathleen take over the solarium at the house as her work area, partly from her own desire to watch the creations come to life under Kathleen's skilled hands. Two young seamstresses now answered to Kathleen and laughter and gaiety filled the house. Occasionally Kathleen would be gifted with a ticket to a performance, which she always passed on to Bea in gratitude for her support (although what Bea *really* wanted was a gown made by Kathleen). "Now dear, don't you want to be sitting in the audience seeing your handicraft on stage?" she would ask, but Kathleen always demurred that she could see them from the wings and was content with that.

A Shakespearean troupe enlisted Kathleen's skills to dress all six leading members of a production that would be presented both in Dublin and London, so Kathleen recruited another talented seamstress and the solarium at Castle Wellington was engulfed in a flurry of activity night and day for a month. When opening night came, Kathleen took her position in the wings with the wardrobe mistress and Bea her seat in the first mezzanine. The play received ovation after ovation, and Kathleen was astonished when she heard her own name announced. The director wanted her to come center stage and accept the applause for her costuming! Kathleen so proud that at least one person she knew, Bea, could see her achievement, yet sad at the same time that so many of the people she had cared about never would.

When the show's run at Dublin came to an end, the director invited Kathleen to his office. When she entered, he was sitting at his desk toying with an envelope in front of him. "Ah, Miss Evans, thank you so much for coming."

"The pleasure is mine, sir."

"Your costumes truly elevated this show and I am certain that the more, well, sophisticated audiences in London will agree." He turned the envelope around and around and Kathleen felt certain it probably held a bonus of some sort. "Which is why I would like to ask you to come to London with the troupe, to make any adjustments that might be necessary," and now he thrust the envelope at Kathleen. "I have taken the liberty of securing passage for you and an assistant, and of course, we will compensate you for your time spent there, perhaps a month if you can?"

London! She had dreamed of going there to see Viola again and to thank Arthur for his opening the world to her that she had always hoped for. "Oh, I can, I can," she stammered. She began calculating just how long it would take to finish the dresses she had on order for an upcoming formal ball. "I'm so honored although I don't know why you'd need me, you have the wardrobe staff and all," she said, hoping he would contradict her, which he did.

"This will be good for the staff, too, the opportunity to learn more from you, Miss Evans. We sail four weeks hence."

Kathleen left the theater and hurried home through the darkened streets. She hoped Bea was still up to share the splendid news. Which seamstress would she take as an assistant? What would she herself wear? Should she write to Arthur first or just surprise them? She had received letters sporadically from Viola, first from a boarding school in the English countryside, later from one in France, and most recently from an academy in Spain. Viola always included drawings that were increasingly sophisticated, but her message was always the same: 'I'm lonely. I don't have anyone who understands me the way you did.' The letters broke Kathleen's heart, but she knew the broad education Viola was receiving would make her life so much more fulfilling in the long run.

Bea was, of course, wholly supportive of Kathleen going to London for as long as she was needed; Bea would keep her rooms just as they were for her return. But she admonished Kathleen, "Now don't use all your time finishing dresses for other women who have dozens of them—make yourself some stunning gowns. I just know Arthur and Vivian will want to take you to balls and parties, and you simply must shine!"

Kathleen had to agree but the fantasies just made her want to work all the faster.

25.

Vicente was right. Jack was handily elected as the next governor of Nevada, easily beating candidates from the more populous cities in the state. His plain-spoken directness had earned him the respect of the average working man as well as the industrialists and entrepreneurs who were becoming more numerous in the western desert state. Jack accepted the victory in stride in his usual laconic way. "I expect folks figure I won't make any bigger mess out of things down there in Carson City," he told his friends at the Delta.

He hadn't even thought about the fact that he would have to move into the newly-built Governor's Mansion, but the widow Drake had — she already had a small sign made for the front yard of the Blake Mansion, "Former residence of Governor Bartley." She was certain it would attract even higher quality boarders. The truth was, she was a different woman ever since the night at Piper's Opera House. Jack had seen her go back-stage with the tenor after the performance and thought to himself at the time, if the tenor joined up with the widow he'd probably be singing an entire octave higher. It turned out the tenor was so besotted with the widow that he didn't even notice that his pianist refused to rehearse during the morning hours, or the afternoon, for that matter. He spent every spare minute with the widow, insisting she take a room at his expense at the Comstock Hotel. However, after three sold-out performances, he was committed to leave Virginia City and return East to perform in four more cities before returning to Italy.

Jack expected she would lord it over the other women in the boarding house at their Sunday dinner, but she was uncharacteristically reserved and also more compassionate with the other women, though not necessarily with Jack whom she still "coached" in the ways of becoming a gentleman. "I worry about you, Governor," she started one evening as they sat on the house's broad verandah, "with no one to watch over you in the Governor's Mansion."

"Oh, I'm sure you'll drop in, won't you, to see how things are?" Jack took the widow's hand. She blushed and told him in no uncertain terms that visitors should not be allowed to 'drop in' at the mansion. Then she truly surprised him.

"I believe I may sell our old house here — we'll split the proceeds, of course. I have decided to return to the continent, perhaps travel to Spain, or even Italy which I have never seen."

Jack smiled. "I think if that's what you want, then you should do it soon as you can." He still held her hand. "You're a damn fine woman and you've been the best to me as anyone." As Vicente had pointed out to Jack sometime back, he was walled-off in some respects but also given to bouts of big emotion. He was having one now as he thought of the genuine friendships and respect he had received since arriving in Virginia City. It was something he never expected to have again after leaving the Army and going through his shameful boxing days. He had enjoyed his one true love early in his life and never would have another, he felt certain, but the other things had made up for it, all in all. When the fireworks show went off signaling Nevada Day, he couldn't help but smile.

26.

Just before Kathleen sailed for London, she delivered a final batch of costumes to the opera in Dublin, arriving rather late in the evening on a night not scheduled for a performance. She was out of breath as she hurried in the side door reserved for musicians and employees. The stage manager jumped up to relieve her of her burden of dresses and jackets. "Oh, I'm so happy you're still here," Kathleen said, short of breath. "I thought I might have carted these down here to find the door locked!"

"Quite the contrary, my dear," the manager said, stacking the costumes on a table. "We have just been treated to the most extraordinary evening of music. I'm so sorry you missed it!"

"I thought the orchestra had the night off," Kathleen said, gently rearranging the freshly-pressed costumes.

"They do, of course, of course, but in walks this chap straight off the street, and presumes to sit down at our piano." The manager pointed to a Steinway center stage. "Without a word he began to play the most marvelous Chopin any of us have ever heard." He sighed. "He played for more than an hour and brought us nearly to tears."

"How strange indeed." Kathleen's brow furrowed. "What did this chap look like? Did he ever talk at all?"

"Just at the end, he bid us a good evening, clearly from the States, and handsome, oh my."

"Go on, Simon, please."

"Well, for starters, long blonde hair in perfect waves, beautifully tapered hands and the bluest eyes, set off by skin like milk." The manager nearly swooned but Kathleen felt a shiver down her spine. But, it couldn't be, could it? He had exactly described the stranger who Viola had felt 'watched over' Kathleen. She put the thought out of her mind. If Philip were in Dublin, surely he would have searched her out, she rationalized. And, his playing, while always competent, was truthfully never dazzling as this night's performance must have been.

Philip was indeed in Dublin, although only for one more evening and only in hopes of covertly observing Kathleen which he had done the previous night as she flew around the solarium supervising her growing staff of seamstresses. He noted the color in her cheeks and the easy way she laughed with the women. She was clearly happy, all he ever really wanted for her, he had to admit. He left for London on the overnight sailing, thinking perhaps he would order a sequined jacket for the stage from her in the future.

Waiting for Philip in London was Vicente, still smoking cigars and reveling in the more sophisticated tobaccos to be found there. He had seen that his protégé could be trusted and even admired, and when Philip got a chance to tour with the London symphony, Vicente decided to tag along. With Jack ensconced in the governor's mansion and Juliette years in the grave, the little mining town of Virginia City appeared to hold no further adventures for the elder vampire.

Kathleen was terribly disappointed when she arrived in London only to learn from the McDougall's that Viola was currently studying in Paris, but they reassured her that Viola's talent was increasing with every new school and that Viola herself, while still headstrong, seemed increasingly confident. Arthur confessed that Viola was really too much for Vivian and himself to handle, hence the series of boarding schools, but he maintained that the outcome was positive, although he said Viola rarely came home to London anymore. As usual, he was working his behind-the-scenes magic on Viola's behalf, putting her in touch with gallery owners and other artists in Paris and beyond. Kathleen concluded her visit with the older couple on a poignant note but promised to keep them in her prayers.

Meanwhile, the Shakespearean troupe she had accompanied to London were already in the process of negotiating their next experience in Paris. For weeks, Kathleen did nothing but design new costumes and keep the current ones in good repair, but she couldn't help hoping that the manager would ask her to continue on with them to Paris and another opportunity to see her dear friend. The troupe's performances were so well received in London that their run was extended and then extended again. Kathleen was reassured that Bea would hold her rooms for her in Dublin, but she also held out hope for a trip to Paris.

And finally, it was to happen. After three hectic months in London the troupe manager gathered everyone together in the theater after a performance and announced they would be heading next to Paris, then on to Barcelona. All of the actors would be asked to stay on, he reassured them, but said nothing to Kathleen who waited anxiously in the wings. When the actors had filed out, she approached him hesitantly.

"So, I imagine you'll be wanting me to just pack up all the costumes and…"

"You organize them any way you like dear. After all, you're in charge of them," the manager said hastily. Then seeing her uncertainty, "Of course, you're going with us, I hope?"

"I very much want to, Simon. I just didn't know…"

"Nonsense, you're responsible for much of our success here and your work will be a hit in Paris and Barcelona, too." He hugged Kathleen briefly then shooed her out the stage door.

There was so much work to do in preparation for the new show that time flew and before she knew it Kathleen found herself strolling through the streets of Paris looking for new materials and new designs. It was on one of these outings that she came upon a small art gallery with welcoming pots of red geraniums on the steps. And in the window was a drawing she would have recognized anywhere. She immediately rushed in and caught the owner's attention. "May I see that piece in the window a bit closer," she asked, almost breathless with anticipation. The gallery owner retrieved the small drawing of a shadowy man watching over a young woman at the railing of a ship, and sure enough, in the lower corner was the signature, "V. McD."

"I simply must have this!" Kathleen exclaimed without even knowing the price.

"Ah yes, interesting work. No one knows who the artist is, but pieces like this are turning up in the galleries and are bought almost immediately." He lowered his voice. "The word is that the artist is rather a recluse," and then he leaned even closer to Kathleen, "and more remarkably, it may even be a woman!"

The End

About the Author

Arline Fisher was raised in Carson City, Nevada, and spent many hours in Virginia City, even tracing her family's roots there through a grandfather who worked on the Virginia and Truckee Railroad. She is a journalism graduate from the University of Nevada, Reno, and has worked as a managing editor on several national magazine and book projects, in addition to doing direct-mail marketing and public relations. She makes her home in St. George, Utah.

Thank you dear friends.

My deepest appreciation goes to my very good friends and loyal readers without whom this would never have been possible. Thank you to Vicki Lund, Claudia Reek, Kirsten Ball and Lonna Burress whose unending support and belief in my abilities carried me to the end of this novel and perhaps well into another. Thanks also to my mother for raising me in a reading household and to my father for many trips to Virginia City and lots of tall tales.

Publisher: Arline Fisher
arlinefisher@centurylink.net

Copyright: ©Arline Fisher

This is entirely a work of fiction. The names, characters and incidents portrayed are the work of the author's imagination. Any resemblance to actual persons, living or dead, is entirely coincidental.

ISBN-13:978-0692450451
ISBN-10:069-2450459

All rights reserved. No part of this publication may be reproduced, stored in or introduced into a retrieval system, or transmitted in any form or by any means (electronic, mechanical, by photocopying, recording or otherwise) without the prior written permission of the publisher/author. Please respect the author's rights and purchase only authorized printed or electronic editions.

www.ingramcontent.com/pod-product-compliance
Lightning Source LLC
Chambersburg PA
CBHW071129170626
46809CB00002B/544